Also available from Abigail Strom

The Hart University series

Rikki

Claire

Tamsin

Julia (coming soon)

Contemporary Romance

Tell Me

Show Me

Almost Like Love

Nothing Like Love

Anything But Love

The Millionaire's Wish

Cross My Heart

Waiting for You

Into Your Arms

Winning the Right Brother

TAMSIN

HART UNIVERSITY, BOOK 3

Abigail Strom

This is a work of fiction. Names, characters, places, and incidents are a product of the author's imagination. Locales and public names are sometimes used for atmospheric purposes. Any resemblance to actual people, living or dead, or to businesses, companies, events, institutions, or locales is completely coincidental.

Cover Art © Sarah Hansen, Okay Creations
Book Layout © BookDesignTemplates.com

Tamsin: Hart University, Book 3/ Abigail Strom.
ISBN 978-1943296064

For Tara, who always tells me the truth

PROLOGUE

Tamsin

You know how some people can't be labeled? You can't fit them into a neat little box?

Yeah, that's not me. I've always been easy to label.

Bad girl.

Skank.

Slut.

From the time I was fifteen years old, that's who I've been. Tamsin Shay, Queen of the Sluts.

But hey, at least I'm queen of something. And as realms go, let me tell you, the kingdom of sluts has some pretty awesome people in it.

I'm proud to be their queen.

CHAPTER ONE

Tamsin

The first time I ever saw Daniel Bowman, he stood up for me. He didn't even know me, and he stood up for me.

Not that I needed him to. That's another thing that happened when I was fifteen: I decided I would never, ever wait for someone else to stand up for me.

Because I would always stand up for myself.

"That's her. The skank who goes at it so loud with Oscar I can hear her through the fucking walls."

It was freshman year, and I was at the coffee house in the basement of Heller Hall, caffeinating myself before class. To give the asshole credit, I don't think he meant for me to hear him. I had ear buds in and I was sitting with my back to the rest of the room.

But I did hear him.

I started to turn around. But I hadn't done more than tense up and put my hands on the edge of the table when I heard another voice.

This one was slow and deep and easy—the kind you always hope has a body to match and hardly ever does.

"Couple things wrong with that," the new voice said.

"Yeah? Enlighten me."

"First, don't call women skanks. Not when I'm around."

There was a short silence. Then:

"Are you shitting me? What are you, fucking Galahad?"

"Second, if you're calling a woman a skank because she's loud in bed, that tells me you've never made a woman come so hard she screams. That's on you, man."

I wanted to stand up and cheer. And at the same time, my throat tightened and I felt like crying.

But I didn't cheer or cry. I just listened to the rest of the conversation, which turned into the asshole trying to defend his bedroom skills and Galahad giving him enough rope to hang himself with. Then, when their chairs scraped the floor as they got up to go, I turned my head.

The asshole said something about his next class and headed for the trash can with his empty cup. But Galahad was still at their table, slinging his backpack over one shoulder.

Oh. My. God.

He wasn't my type. I tended to go for guys like Oscar—guys who wore their artsy natures on their sleeves, going for punk or grunge or beatnik, with tats and piercings a major theme. This guy was more of a preppie god in a button-down shirt and khaki pants.

But it wasn't the clothes I was focused on.

He was big—big like my friend Will, who was on the football team—and he had the kind of body that made me wish he wasn't wearing a long-sleeved shirt. He had short black hair and dark blue eyes and—

And he was looking right at me.

It was just for a second. Then, almost before I could be sure our eyes really *had* met, he turned to follow his asshole friend out the door.

The second time I saw Daniel Bowman was in Oscar's dorm.

"That's him," I said, grabbing Oscar's arm and pointing across the dining hall. "The one who thinks you must be good in bed."

I'd told Oscar about the conversation I'd overheard, which of course he'd loved, with the implied shout-out to his woman-pleasing abilities.

"Him? Okay, yeah. His name is Daniel something. He plays football." Oscar paused. "He's a good guy," he said after a moment, almost grudgingly.

That was freshman year. Sophomore year, Oscar dumped me. My friend Claire, who'd just gotten dumped herself, talked me into taking a vow of celibacy for fall semester.

No one thought I'd last more than a week—least of all me. But I ended up sticking with it longer than Claire did.

We both made it through the semester, thus honoring the vow. Once she was free to date again, though, Claire got together with Will . . . while I found out I kind of liked the whole celibacy thing.

Have you ever known—just *known*—that a boyfriend was about to break up with you? However you react when that happens, it's probably better than how *I* used to react.

I'd get desperate. Clingy. I did all the things you're not supposed to do, the stuff your friends tell you under no circumstances *ever* to do.

Calling and texting all the time. Cooking for him and buying him cute little gifts. Trying to be so amazing in bed he'll never leave you for another.

Trying to be the girl he used to want.

I know. Pathetic, right? My friends thought so, too.

He's not worth it, Tamsin.

He doesn't deserve you.

Just focus on yourself. Your classes. The important stuff.

That last piece of advice came from my roommate Rikki, who's amazing. She's always been able to focus on work and classes and "important stuff," even freshman year when the rest of us were floundering around pretending we had it all together. Rikki actually did have it all together, except for this one time when things fell apart with Sam—the guy she's with now. The guy who loves her the way every woman in the world dreams of being loved.

For years I went from guy to guy looking for that, hoping for that, and never ever finding it. But those days or weeks of knowing it was over before it actually *was* over were the worst.

And then, like magic, things changed.

Maybe it was having a friend do the vow-of-celibacy thing with me. Maybe I'd finally hit some kind of critical mass of shitty boyfriends. Whatever the reason, something changed that semester.

The fever broke. And God, the relief.

No more lying awake at night wondering what I'd done wrong, wondering when he'd call, or wondering if he'd stick around till morning. Guys stopped being the center of my life.

And I will never, ever, *ever* go back to way I used to be.

Just to be clear, though: I'm still Queen of the Sluts. Once a slut, always a slut, even if you've decided you've had enough crappy relationships and want to take a good long break.

It's the first day of junior year, and this is where I am. Stronger than I've ever been, happier than I've ever been. Rikki says I've found an equilibrium for myself, and that feels right.

I looked up equilibrium. The first definitions are 1. *Bodily balance* and 2. *Emotional stability.* I read those two phrases over again and again because I liked them so much.

Nothing, and I mean nothing, will make me give up my bodily balance or emotional stability ever again.

Not even the preppie god who just walked into my Experiments in Drama class.

CHAPTER TWO

Daniel

"I need to take one more arts class before I graduate. I want to get it over with now, so I can focus on my senior project next year. Which one will cause me the least amount of pain?"

I'm in the living room with my two housemates, and we're finalizing our schedules for junior year.

Trace leans over and looks at my computer screen. "These five are your only options?"

"They're the ones that don't have prerequisites. They also fit into my schedule around football and other classes. So, yeah. These five."

Trace is frowning. "Not Experiments in Drama. That one will be full of feminists and social justice warriors. How about Hemingway, Faulkner, and Fitzgerald?"

Beeker shakes his head. "Gotta disagree with Mr. Men's Rights Activist on this one. Experiments in Drama will be full of girls with no inhibitions and the guys will all be gay. Statistically speaking, you're not going to find better odds."

Trace looks disgusted. "Never fuck a feminist. You'll just get accused of rape the next day. Unless you want to ask for consent every ten seconds. 'I'd like to take off your shirt. Do you consent? I'd like to touch your breast. Do you consent? I'd like to—'"

"Shut up."

My voice is harsh, and Trace looks surprised. But on this particular issue I'm with the feminists. Consent is black and white. It's not something I ever joke about, and I don't stay quiet if someone else jokes about it, either. Including a housemate.

Trace and Beeker and I all go to the same church, and we decided to get a place together last year. At the time, I thought it was a great idea. I was psyched to live with people who share my values. People who believe in God, who do volunteer work, who want to make the world a better place. But lately, I've been starting to wonder if Trace and I really *do* share values—or just a church.

Trace levers himself up from the beat up old couch and heads for the kitchen. He mutters "Galahad" as he goes, but I don't call him on it.

It's been a while since I've heard that nickname. It dogged me freshman year after a guy in my dorm stuck it on me, but it faded away sophomore year.

I hate it. I try to be a decent person and live a decent life, but you don't do good things hoping to get praised for them. Whenever I hear "Galahad" it makes me think of someone who wears virtue like a suit of armor, showing off how pure of heart he is. Someone holier-than-thou.

I don't want to be that guy.

"What's with Trace?" Beeker asks. "He's been in a bad mood for days."

I shake my head. "No idea."

"Well, fuck him." Beeker waves a hand at my computer. "And take Experiments in Drama. Not just because it'll be a good dating pool, but because it won't be any work. Acting stuff, right? No essays or exams or anything."

That's a selling point. I've got some tough courses this semester and I could use an easy class on my schedule.

Plus, I have a deep dark secret. I used to do the Christmas pageant at my church back home. The show was as cheesy as you'd expect and none of us were great actors or anything, but the first year I did it there was this moment that . . . I don't know.

I was playing Joseph. I rehearsed dutifully for the three weeks before Christmas, but I was pretty bored by the whole thing. Then, when we showed up at church to perform on Christmas Eve, there were all these candles.

Hundreds of candles.

Something about the candlelight and the smell of frankincense and myrrh—someone had brought in the real thing for us to use that night—kind of got to me. It made the cheap set and costumes seem real. And for a moment—a couple of minutes, maybe—I actually felt like Joseph. I wanted to take care of Mary and the baby, and do my best to be a good man. And I was overwhelmed by the light of God.

Okay, that sounds as cheesy as the show was. But it's true.

Anyway, I sign up for Experiments in Drama. I don't know if it's the acting thing or the no homework thing that tips the scale, but it's not the dating prospect thing.

Because here's another deep dark secret.

I'm a virgin. I've dated and I've fooled around, but I haven't had sex yet.

That was okay in high school and when I was a freshman. But sometime last year, girls started to think it was weird that I didn't want to sleep with them. By the end of spring semester, I stopped dating and fooling around because I didn't want to talk about why I wouldn't do more.

I know there are girls out there who haven't had sex yet and aren't ready to. Maybe I'll meet one of those girls this year and get back to fooling around.

But until then, I'm not looking to date.

I know where my focus will be this semester. Football. Engineering. Church. Community service.

And Tuesdays and Thursdays at 7:30 pm, Experiments in Drama.

CHAPTER THREE

Tamsin

Daniel Bowman is taking an acting class?

I've been looking forward to Experiments in Drama all summer. It's open to juniors without any prerequisites, but most of the people who take it are drama majors. The professor is supposed to be amazing and I really want to stretch myself this semester. Take risks, delve deep, all that.

It's an evening class, too, which is good. I'm not a morning person. My night performances have always been better than my matinees, and I'm hoping I'll improv better at night, too. Plus the class is in a theater, which is fun. We'll meet in the small, student-run space where they do smaller shows, experimental stuff, and open-mic events. A very cool environment.

Then, as I'm sitting here thinking about flexing my acting muscles, in walks Daniel Bowman.

Now, I should get something straight. Just because I've been celibate for almost a year doesn't mean my lady parts have stopped working. And the sight of Daniel Bowman makes everything down there tingle.

As I've mentioned, I usually go more for grunge than clean-cut. But something about Daniel's squeaky clean appearance turns my crank. He looks like he just got out of the shower after working out at the gym, and I want to rip open that blue button-down shirt and unzip those pressed gray trousers and—

"It is a truth universally acknowledged: the hotter a guy is, the worse he is in bed."

I glance at Izzy. Sure enough, she's looking right at Daniel, who's standing in the doorway peering around in the dim light of the theater.

His neat dark hair invites a serious mussing, and he's sporting an equally neat beard and mustache. Then, of course, there's the truly impressive body filling out his business casual clothes. He's looking a little confused, maybe because it's dark in the theater and his eyes are adjusting, but more likely because he doesn't belong here.

"It's also a truth universally acknowledged that guys who look like that don't take drama classes," I remind Izzy. "No offense," I add to Charlie, who's sitting on her other side.

Charlie, his eyes on his Twitter feed, doesn't even bother to look up.

"None taken. Besides, isn't the implication that I'm good in bed? Which I am."

I turn back toward Daniel and raise my voice. "Unless you're looking for Experiments in Drama, you're in the wrong place."

Daniel looks up at me. Charlie, Izzy and I are sitting about halfway up the raked seating area, with another dozen or so students scattered around us. We're all facing the small stage, waiting for our professor, Joan Washington, to make an appearance.

"Experiments in Drama," he repeats, in the slow, deep, sexy voice I remember from freshman year. "Yeah, that's where I need to be."

He stares at me for a moment, and the tingling in my nether regions gets a little more intense. Then he starts walking up the stairs, and I wonder if he's going to take the open seat next to me.

My heart starts to pound.

But about three rows below us he stops and takes the seat on the aisle, setting his backpack on the floor. He leans over, unzips the backpack, and pulls out a notebook and pen.

Now for the real question. What the hell is he doing in this class?

He's an engineering major. He's also on the football team, although he's not a starter. I started watching games last year because of my friends Will and Andre, and I learned that Daniel Bowman is a backup tight end. Whatever that is.

"He's a decent player and a really good guy. Solid, you know? Dependable. Just not first string material."

That's what Andre said when I asked about Daniel last year. Not first string material.

To be honest, that sounds a little bit like me. I auditioned for the lead role in five different shows last year, and I was cast as a supporting character three times and an understudy twice.

This year, I'm going to change that. I'm going to make myself into lead actor material, and I'm going to make other people see me that way, too.

Izzy nudges me. "What's up?" she whispers. "You've got this intense scowl on your face. Do you know that guy?"

I *am* frowning. After a moment, I realize why.

I don't want anything to distract me from my goals this semester. I don't want distractions in this class in particular.

And I'm worried that Daniel Bowman has the potential to be one huge-ass distraction.

"He's in the engineering department," I whisper back. "He's on the football team. He's definitely not a drama major. I'm just trying to figure out why he's in this class."

"There aren't any prerequisites. Maybe he figured it would be an easy way to knock out his arts requirement." She shrugs. "Anyway, he's hot. You used to appreciate having eye candy around."

It's true. I did. Even when you're not eating, you can still enjoy reading off the menu.

It's just that a guy as fine as Daniel Bowman can make you feel like you're starving. And when you're starving, it's hard to think about anything but food.

But I'm not going to explain all of that to Izzy right now. And anyway, it won't be an issue. I was just surprised to see Daniel here, that's all. All I have to do is ignore him. Stay focused. Don't get distrac—

"Sex."

The voice is loud, and seems to come from everywhere. I jump and let out a squeak.

Izzy smacks me on the arm. "What is wrong with you?"

"Who's talking?"

Izzy smacks me again. "Our professor. Who's standing on stage. Now shut up, please."

It's true. Joan Washington is standing on the stage, her hands in her jeans pockets, smiling up at us. And I didn't even see her come in.

Grrrrr. It's already happening! Daniel is distracting me, damn it.

I look down at him. He's sitting there stiff with surprise, his notebook on his knee and his pen poised above a blank page. He seems like the dutiful note-taker type and I wonder if he's going to write down the word "sex".

"How did you feel when I said that?" Professor Washington asks. "Did you react to the word? What happened inside you, viscerally?"

There's some stirring among the students. We're sort of scattered around, and now the professor grins at us.

"Let's bring it in a little. Come on down, okay? First and second rows, please."

We all get to our feet and shuffle down to the two front rows. In the scrum, I end up sitting between Izzy and Daniel.

He's on my right. He smells like soap and mint—toothpaste or shampoo, I don't know which—and when his thigh brushes mine every muscle in my belly tightens.

I can feel the warmth of his body—unless that's actually a rush of heat I've generated all on my own. I send a quick glance his way and he's looking down at his notebook, frowning. Then he looks up, but not at me. He's looking at our professor, who's come forward to sit on the apron of the stage.

No distractions, I remind myself, and turn my attention the same way.

I've seen Joan Washington around, of course. She's a popular professor in the drama department. But this is the first time I've been in a class of hers.

She looks like Mrs. Claus.

No, really. She's this edgy, avant-garde teacher and director, and she looks like the jolly wife of Santa Claus.

She's in her fifties or sixties, short and plump and rosy-cheeked. She has curly gray hair and a big smile.

Her clothes aren't Christmas-y, of course. She's wearing jeans and a T-shirt with a red panda on it.

I love red pandas.

"Okay, let's try a different word." She pauses. "Love."

She looks at us, and we look back at her.

"Think about your reactions to those two different words. Mentally, emotionally, physically. Store that information for our first exercise. Now find a partner."

I'm caught by surprise. By the time I turn to my left, Izzy and Charlie have already paired up.

That leaves the person on my right.

I turn to Daniel. "Do you want to work together?"

"Sure."

He doesn't sound super enthusiastic. In fact, he sounds downright hesitant. But I'm going to assume that's because he's an engineering major in a drama class and not because he has some kind of problem with me.

"All right," Professor Washington says. "Now find some space, either out there in the audience or up here on stage."

Daniel nods toward the back of the house. "Do you want to go up there?"

"Okay."

We leave our backpacks but Daniel takes his notebook and pen. He steps out into the aisle and then waits for me to precede him up the stairs, which is a kind of politeness I'm not used to.

I go up to the back row and take a seat, and Daniel sits down next to me.

As we turn toward each other our knees touch, and both of us scoot back from the contact.

I clear my throat.

"I'm Tamsin."

"I know. You're friends with Andre, right? We're teammates."

I nod.

"I'm Daniel," he says.

"I know. You were in my boyfriend's dorm freshman year."

It's too dark up here to tell for sure, but I think his face turns a little red. Then again, maybe that's just my imagination.

"All right, everyone, here's the exercise. You're going to ask each other questions about those two words. Love and sex. You can ask anything you want, and there's only one rule for your answers. You can't lie. You can say you won't answer, but if you do answer it has to be the truth. Okay, go."

Jeepers.

Normally I jump right into acting exercises, but this time I think I'll wait for my partner to go first.

But after a long silence, I figure it's up to the actual theater major to get things started.

"Have you ever been in love?" I ask.

He hesitates a moment before answering. "No."

I stare at him. "You've never been in love?"

"No."

I know he's dated a few girls at Hart, but at the moment I can only think of one name.

"So . . . Bree Simms? You weren't in love with her?"

He shakes his head. "I cared about her. I really liked her. But I wasn't in love with her." He pauses. "Okay, my turn."

"Sure."

"Have you ever been in love?"

"God, yes. Falling in love is my fatal weakness."

He raises one eyebrow, which is a really sexy look on him.

"Love is a weakness?"

"Only when they don't love you back."

Now both eyebrows go up. "Come on, Tamsin."

"What?"

"You can't expect me to believe the guys you've been in love with haven't loved you back."

"I can't? Why not?"

He gestures toward me. "Look at you."

Warmth spirals up inside me, and I hope Daniel can't see how much I like his compliment.

I figure the safest refuge is humor.

"You don't have to tell me I'm good-looking. I've got a mirror. But it takes more than a pretty face for someone to fall in love with you."

"Yeah, but you—" He stops.

"I what?"

"Nothing."

"Come on, finish the thought. Were you going to say I have many loveable qualities? Based on not knowing me at all?"

He smiles at that, and it turns out his smile is as sexy as his eyebrow-raising.

"Call it an instinct."

"Your instincts tell you I'm loveable?"

"Yeah." He pauses. "Are you in love with someone right now?"

"No. I've gone cold-turkey on my big weakness."

"You've gone cold-turkey on love?"

"Love, relationships, dating, all of it. I'm coming up on a year of celibacy."

I'm not sure exactly why I revealed that. Am I letting him know I'm not on the market, or am I reminding myself?

"My turn," I say now.

"Okay."

I cast around for something good to ask. We've already covered love, so maybe it's time for sex.

"What's your favorite thing to do in bed with someone?"

He blinks. "Uh . . ."

"You can choose not to answer," I remind him. "Of course if you do, I'll tease you unmercifully for being a coward."

"You will, huh? A fate worse than death." He pauses a moment. "Oral."

Having dated a few guys in my time, this comes as no surprise.

"You like it when a girl goes down on you?"

"No. I like going down on girls."

Now it's my eyebrows shooting up.

"You're not allowed to lie, Daniel."

"I'm not lying."

"Going down on a girl is your favorite thing to do in bed?"

"Yeah."

This deserves a lot more conversation. But at that moment Professor Washington says,

"Okay, everyone, come back to where you were."

In a couple of minutes I'm sitting between Izzy and Daniel again. Only this time, the whole right side of my body is warm.

Professor Washington waits until we've all settled into our seats.

"All right. Now that we've warmed up with a couple of provocative but relatively easy words, let's try something tougher." She pauses. "Abortion."

Wow. Talk about provocative.

"So?" she asks after a moment. "What's your reaction when you hear that word?"

After a moment, Charlie speaks up.

"It makes me uncomfortable."

A few students nod.

"Okay. Why? What's the source of the discomfort?"

Someone else answers that—a student I don't know.

"It's a political issue. A tense one."

A blonde girl sitting in front of me chimes in. "Hearing that word makes me feel angry, because reproductive rights are under assault in this country. And I feel helpless, because we've been fighting for so long."

A lot of nods to that.

Now another girl I don't know. "We all know the issue isn't abortion. It's about men controlling a woman's body. It's about women being seen as baby machines, without any value or agency as human beings outside of that."

As people talk, I start to feel my own anger, too.

"It's like we can't ever relax," I put in. "My grandmother has been going to pro-choice marches for forty-five years, and she wears one of those shirts that says, *I can't believe I still have to protest this shit.*"

That gets a rueful laugh. And then, on my right, Daniel says,

"Wait a minute."

Professor Washington looks at him expectantly. "Yes?"

"Is everyone here pro-choice?"

The blonde girl in front of us twists around to stare at him. "Of course. Aren't you?"

He pauses a second. Then:

"No."

CHAPTER FOUR

Daniel

I've never gotten stink eye like I'm getting it right now.

Everyone is staring at me like I've grown a second head. Even the professor looks a little surprised. But after a few seconds she says,

"Okay, good. The political viewpoints in my classes can tend to be a little, uh, homogenous. Having diverse opinions is a good thing." She looks at everyone else. "What about the rest of you? How many of you would describe yourselves as pro-choice?"

Every single hand goes up, including the hand of the girl next to me.

Tamsin Shay.

I was a freshman when I saw Tamsin for the first time. She was dating a guy in my dorm, and she visited a lot.

Oscar was just a few rooms away from me. I used to leave my door open on the nights Tamsin came over, on the off chance I might catch a glimpse of her walking down the hall.

There's a difference between beautiful and sexy. Tamsin Shay is both.

I used to get so pissed at the way Oscar took her for granted that I wished I could fight him over her, like a medieval knight dueling for a lady's honor. But he was a scrawny guy, and even if he'd been the Rock I didn't really have an excuse to take him on.

Except that I had a crush on his girlfriend.

She and Oscar broke up at some point, which meant she stopped coming to the dorm. I still saw her around, though, since she was friends with Will McKenna and Andre Arceneaux. Will was my teammate for two years and Andre still is. Even though I don't hang with those guys outside of football, I see Tamsin sometimes when she meets up with Andre after practice or a game.

And my blood still goes south whenever I do.

Just like it did tonight when I walked into this theater. And just like it did when we were sitting together in the back row, talking about love and sex.

Now she's sitting next to me with her hand in the air, along with every other student in here, looking at me like I'm an alien.

I'm starting to think it might have been Trace, and not Beeker, who was right about this class.

I look at the professor. "Can I ask something?"

"Of course."

I never make a decision without doing at least a little research, and the same was true for Experiments in Drama. I looked up student comments about last year's class to see what I'd be getting into.

"Last year you focused on Greek drama. Euripides and Aristophanes."

The professor nods. "Yes, that's right. What's your question?"

I thought it was obvious, but I guess not.

"What does abortion have to do with theater and acting? Why are we even talking about this?"

Professor Washington is sitting on the edge of the stage, and now she pulls up her legs to sit cross-legged. I've never seen a woman who looks so much like a grandmother sit like that.

"Well," she says, "every class is different. Two years ago, we did musical theater and I made everyone learn how to tap dance. This year we'll be exploring the role of politics in drama. More than that, though. We're going to explore what makes politics personal, how the personal can become political, and how that makes people uncomfortable." She grins at me. "Like you are right now."

"I'm not uncomfortable," I say quickly.

But that's just a reflex. A guy who doesn't drink or do drugs gets into plenty of situations where he feels uncomfortable, and my policy is to say *I'm not uncomfortable* whether or not it's true. Not for myself so much as for everyone around me. So *they* don't feel uncomfortable.

This time, though, it's as much for me as anyone else. You're not supposed to talk about politics in public. The only place I ever bring up my political views is with Trace and Beeker, or other friends who agree with me.

Trace likes to rant, but even he only does that in our house or after church . . . literally preaching to the choir. Although he does sometimes get into fights on social media.

I've seen how ugly politics can get on Twitter. How much uglier would it be in person?

"If you're not uncomfortable, I'm not doing my job," the professor says now. "If you don't get out of your comfort zone you'll never do your best work."

I assume she's talking about drama, not engineering. Because engineering has never made me uncomfortable.

Who tries to feel uncomfortable on purpose? Other than, I guess, theater kids?

"That's why I'm glad you're in this class, uh—"

"Daniel."

"Daniel. I'm glad you're here, because you'll be able to challenge some of our ideas . . . and more importantly, some of our feelings."

Great. Just what I've always wanted.

"I've got a list of films and TV shows that have dealt with abortion in some way. Your assignment for next time will be to watch at least one and write a journal entry response. Keep it open-ended—your feelings, your thoughts, whatever strikes you."

Well, damn. Not only am I surrounded by pro-choice feminists—just like Trace said I'd be—but there *is* going to be work in this class.

For a couple minutes, while Professor Washington takes a stack of handouts from her briefcase and starts to pass them around, I think seriously about dropping Experiments in Drama.

But then Tamsin reaches over, grabs the pen and notebook out of my hands, and starts writing something.

I'm frozen in place after that. Because our hands brushed, and as she leaned toward me her dark wavy hair floated past my face.

I got a whiff of her shampoo. It's sweet and spicy at the same time.

It doesn't take her long to finish writing, and then she shoves the notebook back at me.

R U seriously pro-life? Seriously?

I sigh, take the pen from her, and write.

Yeah. A lot of people are. Why are you so shocked? Have you never met a pro-life person before?

I hold the notebook so she can see it. She reads what I wrote, frowning, her lips pressed together. She's wearing dark red lipstick, and even though I don't usually like heavy makeup on girls, on Tamsin it's sexy as hell.

And it's way too easy to imagine blood-red lip marks on my face, my neck, my chest.

She takes the notebook back, still frowning, and this time when she writes I can see she's settling in for a paragraph at least.

The handouts come my way and I take two, one for me and one for Tamsin. I look down at the list of movies and TV shows but I'm not really reading it.

Finally Tamsin hands the notebook back.

I overheard you talking with some asshole freshman year. You seemed really sex-positive in that conversation. I don't understand how someone with that kind of attitude toward women could be opposed to them making their own healthcare decisions.

I suppose I should be coming up with a pro-life argument. But instead, I'm looking back on freshman year, trying to think of what conversation Tamsin could be talking about.

Maybe the direct approach is best.

What conversation are you talking about?

But before Tamsin can write an answer, Professor Washington comes to sit at the edge of the stage again.

"Now it's time to experiment with some drama. That's the name of this class, right? Who's up for improv?"

Everyone's hand goes up except for mine. So naturally, she calls on me.

"Daniel, let's start with you. Who's going to be his scene partner?"

Everyone raises their hand again, and the professor calls on Tamsin. I'm still just sitting, not sure what to do, when Tamsin elbows me in the ribs.

"Go up there," she hisses at me.

And then, before I know what the hell is happening, Tamsin and I are climbing the steps that lead to the stage while Professor Washington is hopping down and taking a seat in the front row.

This is a whole lot different from playing Joseph in a church play. For one thing, there's no script.

My gut tightens. Sweat prickles under my arms.

Tamsin, on the other hand, is totally calm. She's looking down at Professor Washington, waiting for instructions.

"All right, here's the setup. Tamsin, you're a mother taking your daughter to a clinic for an abortion. Daniel, you're an anti-abortion protestor outside the clinic. Questions?"

Yes! I have questions! How the hell does this work? What am I supposed to do or say? I've never improvised on a stage in front of people before. How do I—

"No questions," Tamsin says.

Shit.

CHAPTER FIVE

Tamsin

I'm as fired up with adrenaline as I've ever been on a stage. Maybe it's stupid to feel betrayed, but I do. For two years I've had this idea of Daniel as some kind of defender of women's sexual self-determination, and now it turns out he doesn't even think women should have power over their own bodies.

It just goes to show: you can't ever trust a guy who's that good-looking. There's always some kind of catch.

But while it's okay to let emotion fuel your acting—in fact it's the first rule of good acting—I can't let this get personal. I want theater to be my profession, and that means behaving professionally.

Just act your ass off, Tamsin.

Okay, Voice Inside My Head. I will.

"Begin scene," Professor Washington says.

I turn on Daniel. He's a lot bigger than I am—like, a *lot*—but I don't feel small.

"Get out of my way."

He's got a deer-in-the-headlights look, and I wonder how much improv he's done in his life. Which brings me back to the question of why he's even in this class.

Or it would bring me back to that question, if I wasn't acting my ass off and not letting things get personal.

"I—"

I take a step toward him. "How dare you try to shame and intimidate my daughter."

"I—"

"It's easy for you, isn't it? Carrying a sign that says 'Choose Life' when you don't know anything about our lives."

I gesture toward the imaginary sign I've just invented, and he actually looks up at it. His hands even shape themselves as though they're holding it.

He's got a few improv instincts, at least.

He looks back at me, still holding the invisible sign, and I see the muscles of his throat jump as he swallows.

"It's true, I don't know you or your daughter. I don't know anything about your lives. But I know you *are* alive. Don't you want your unborn grandchild to have that gift? The gift of being born?"

"When my daughter decides she's ready to have a child—*if* she chooses to have a child—she'll bring a baby into this world who's wanted. A baby she's ready to care for and raise. But she's sixteen years old right now, and she's not ready for any of that."

Daniel frowns. "She made the decision to have sex. Shouldn't she take responsibility for that decision? Actions have consequences."

My spine goes rigid and my nostrils flare. I've never been pregnant myself, but one of my closest friends in high school had an abortion and it's her experience I draw on now.

"Why aren't you saying that to the guy who got her pregnant?"

"Because—" He stops.

I take another step toward him, and now I'm pretty much in his face.

"That's right. You're not saying any of that crap to the guy who got her pregnant because *he isn't here.* He doesn't have to be. He's not pregnant. Do you know what he told my daughter when he found out? *Your baby. Your problem.*"

"Okay, that's—that's obviously not—I mean, that sucks. That's terrible. But if you prove paternity he'd have to—"

"What? Pay child support?"

"Yes."

"Would he have to face what my daughter would have to face? The reality teen mothers face? Less school, worse job prospects, worse health, worse quality of life?

Would he risk death if the pregnancy turns out to be medically dangerous? Could he be legally forced to raise the child, care about the child, care about the mother? Could he be forced to be a father?"

"I don't—"

I take a deep breath. "We live in a world where men can walk away from the consequences of their actions. Thank God we also live in a world where women can take control of their own lives, by deciding when and if they bring a child into this world."

And then, for the first time in my life, an audience bursts into spontaneous applause—for me.

"Okay, end scene," Professor Washington says, as the cheering dies down. "Good job, both of you—but I think we know where the intensity was in that one. Don't worry, Daniel, you'll get another bite at this apple. The two of you will start us off next time. The rest of you, find a scene partner before Thursday's class. I won't tell you what the setups will be, so be ready for anything." She glances at her watch. "Okay, that's it for today. Don't forget your journal entries for next time."

Adrenaline is still pumping through my system.

Where did all that anger come from? I'm pro-choice, but I've never been an activist or anything. Was it acting or something else that came out of me just now?

Daniel and I make our way off the stage and back to our seats. I half expect him to say something to me about our scene, but he just grabs his backpack and heads for the door.

Izzy leans toward me. "Even money says he's not back next time."

"You think he'll drop the class?"

"Yeah. I mean, imagine the reverse."

"The reverse?"

Izzy nods. "Picture yourself at a church in Utah or Alabama or someplace, surrounded by pro-lifers. Would you stick around?"

Charlie says something to Izzy then, and the two of them start talking. But I don't listen, because Izzy's comment is making me think.

Does Daniel feel like that? Like he's surrounded by a hostile army?

Well, why shouldn't he? Women have been facing a hostile army on the subject of abortion for decades. And the stakes are a lot higher for us than him.

But . . .

I don't want to win the argument by drowning him out or running him out of town. I want to win the argument because my argument is better.

And I want to know how the guy who said the stuff he did freshman year could possibly oppose a woman's right to choose.

But I'm guessing Izzy's prediction is accurate. I'm guessing Daniel won't show up for our next class.

And my feelings about all this are so confused I don't even know if I'm relieved or sorry.

On my way out I realize I left my backpack behind. I tell Izzy and Charlie I'll catch up with them and go back to get it.

Because of that, I'm the last person to leave the theater. It's on the basement level of the performing arts building, and the hallway outside is dimly lit and a little chilly. I'm hurrying toward the warmth that waits for me outside when Daniel Bowman, waiting in the shadows under the stairwell, steps in front of me.

"What conversation?" he says.

My heart skips a beat.

He doesn't look mad, but he looks intense. He's frowning and his arms are folded, which draws attention to how broad his shoulders are.

Damn, he's good looking. And tall. And . . .

"I'm sorry," I say after a moment. "What did you say?"

He unfolds his arms and slides his hands into the pockets of those neatly pressed trousers.

"You said you overheard a conversation of mine freshman year. You said I was sex-positive or some other feminist thing."

He uses the word *feminist* like it's an insult instead of a compliment, which is irritating. But I can deal with that later.

"It was in the coffee house at Heller Hall. Some guy from your dorm called me a skank because he could hear me and my boyfriend—Oscar—having sex through the walls. And you told him—"

I swallow. Two years later, and I still remember what it felt like to have a total stranger defending me. And now it looks like I'm going to find out he never meant to defend me at all. Or something.

"You told him not to call women skanks. And you said if he called a woman a skank for being loud in bed, it just meant he never made a woman come so hard she screams."

Daniel is still staring at me, and his frown slowly fades away until his forehead is smooth again.

"I remember that conversation," he says after a moment.

Thank God for that, anyway. At least he doesn't think I'm making it up.

"I didn't realize you heard us talking," he continues. "I'm sorry."

What's he apologizing for? Standing up for me?

"What do you mean, you're sorry? Sorry for what?"

"Sorry that Shane was such a prick. And that you had to listen to his bullshit."

And just like that, my throat starts to ache and tears sting behind my eyelids.

"That's nice of you," I say gruffly.

We continue staring at each other, and I'm damned if I can remember why we even started talking about this.

But Daniel remembers.

"So. What does that have to do with me being prolife?"

Right.

I take a breath. "You didn't slut-shame me. Another feminist phrase, if you're keeping track. Like sex-positive. Which you also were. So if you respect women making choices about when and how they have sex and who they have it with, why don't you respect a woman's right to make decisions about her uterus?"

That brings the frown back. He pulls his hands from his pockets and folds his arms again.

"Why is it all about her rights? Who's looking out for the rights of the unborn child?"

"A fertilized egg isn't a child. It's a bunch of cells."

His frown deepens.

"Have you ever seen an ultrasound picture of a fetus?"

"Of course I have."

"Then how can you say it's not a child?"

"Because it can't survive outside the womb. And because most abortions are performed in the first eight weeks, when it's an embryo and not a fetus." I take a deep breath. "And what about the woman? She's more than a baby incubator. She's actually a person. A real, live person. Why don't you care what *she* wants?"

"I—"

But I'm on a roll now. "And what do you propose to do if a woman wants an abortion after you make it illegal? Are you going to chain her to a wall or something? Force her to give birth against her will? One in four women will have an abortion in their lifetime. That's a lot of people to chain up, Daniel. Is that really what you want?"

My voice is loud enough to echo in the empty hallway, but Daniel doesn't back down.

"Of course that's not what I want." He's getting louder, too. "That's a stupid straw man argument. Do you think they chained women up before Roe v. Wade?"

I take a step toward him, just like I did when we were doing our scene. "No. You know what happened before Roe v. Wade? Women still had abortions. Hundreds of thousands a year. Only they were illegal, and dangerous. Is *that* what you want? You want us to go back to the coat hanger days?"

"No! Stop putting words in my mouth. I just want unborn babies to have a chance to live. The same chance you and I got."

"But you can't talk about unborn babies and just forget about the women carrying them. And you can't pretend that women will stop getting abortions if Roe v.

Wade is overturned. They'll just happen in back alleys, like they used to. If you want to stop abortions, provide free birth control. Teach kids about safe sex and preventing pregnancy. Or are you one of those abstinence-only assholes?"

Daniel's jaw is tense, and his eyes are glittering in the fluorescent light. "Actually, no. I believe in sex ed and birth control and teaching kids to have safe sex. But if that doesn't work—if a couple gets pregnant anyway—then don't you think, just maybe, that's part of God's plan?"

I stare at him. "Oh, damn."

"What?"

"You're one of those. A religious nut."

It's his turn to take a step toward me.

"And you're one of *those.*"

"One of what?"

"An intolerant liberal. An anti-religious bigot."

I put my hands on my hips. My chin is already up. As far as aggressors go, I probably resemble a small angry rooster facing a big angry dog.

But you never see the rooster back down.

"I *am* a liberal. But I'm not intolerant, and I'm not anti-religious. I just don't want your religion anywhere near my constitutional rights."

"The right to an abortion isn't enshrined in the constitution."

"Tell that to the Supreme Court justices who decided Roe v. Wade in 1973."

"Supreme Courts have made shitty rulings before. Remember Dred Scot?"

"Oh my God. You can't seriously be comparing the Dred Scot decision to—"

"Are you guys practicing a scene? Or is this for real?"

Daniel and I jerk our heads around at the sound of Izzy's voice.

She's standing in the hallway a few yards away. I remember now that I told her and Charlie I'd catch up with them.

How much time has gone by since then?

I take a deep breath. "Sorry, Iz. I'll be out in a second, okay?"

Izzy looks curious, but she just nods, turns, and heads toward the exit. Daniel and I watch until the door closes behind her.

Once she's gone, we look at each other again. Daniel's expression is different now. The anger is gone, replaced by uncertainty.

I feel uncertain too. Our argument got so intense so fast.

"Goodbye," I say finally, the word sounding too abrupt and too loud.

I turn to follow Izzy out of the building. But before I can take more than a couple of steps, Daniel reaches out and touches my shoulder.

I'm not ready for what happens to my body. Goose bumps prickle every inch of my skin and my heart starts to pound.

I turn back to face him.

"I stand by what I said," he tells me.

Great. So he's not letting go of the argument even after—

"There's nothing wrong with a woman enjoying sex. That's how it's supposed to be. And any guy who says otherwise is an asshole."

It's obvious he means it. But how does his no slut-shaming policy tie in to his religious beliefs? Not to mention the whole pro-life thing?

My emotions feel tangled. Underneath everything else, a part of me wants to solve the riddle of this man. To figure out what makes him tick.

But I doubt I'll have the chance.

"You're going to drop this class, aren't you?" I say.

He frowns. "Why do you think that?"

I shrug. "I don't know. If I was in a class surrounded by right wing nut jobs, I'd probably drop it."

He grins suddenly.

"No you wouldn't. You'd stay and take them on."

Man, that smile. It's lopsided and warm and sexy as hell, and a bunch of other things that make my stomach muscles tighten.

"Well. If you're not going to drop the class, I guess I'll see you Thursday."

Then I turn and hurry away.

CHAPTER SIX

Daniel

I can't stop thinking about Tamsin.

It's Wednesday afternoon, and I'm at football practice. As I lurch to my feet after a brutal hit by Andre—it's his job to take me out of every play—Coach finally calls a five-minute water break.

"Hey," I say to Andre as we grab bottles from the ice bucket. "You know Tamsin Shay, right?"

Andre nods. "She's a friend."

I chug water and wipe my mouth with the back of my hand.

"What's her story? I heard she's been single for a while."

Andre and I aren't close or anything, but we respect each other. I figure he knows I'm not a player when it comes to girls, and that I'm not just looking to get laid.

But still, he stares at me for a few seconds before he answers.

"Why are you asking?"

Shit. Is it possible Andre has a thing for Tamsin?

"Hey, man. If I'm stepping on your toes, I—"

"No. That's not it." He shifts his helmet from one hand to the other. "It's just that I don't think you guys are types."

Types?

It's early September, hot and humid, and I'm soaked with sweat. I wipe my face with a towel and look at Andre again.

"What do you mean?"

Andre looks at me kind of appraisingly.

"I don't want to piss you off," he says.

"You won't."

"It's just . . . well, you're a really nice guy, Bowman."

"Is that the part that's going to piss me off?"

He grins. "Well, it would piss off some guys. But you're from, you know, this small town in Kansas or whatever and—"

"Missouri."

"Whatever. And Tamsin is from San Francisco."

I blink. "Dude. Our quarterback is Muslim and his girlfriend is Jewish. Are you seriously talking to me about the great divide between city girls and country boys?"

He grins again. "Okay, fair point. But it's not just the San Francisco thing. I mean . . ." He hesitates. "This is the part that might piss you off. I'm friends with a girl you dated last year. Bree Simms?"

Shit.

I haven't dated anyone since Bree. In fact, Bree is one of the reasons I stopped dating.

I think I know what's coming. "Yeah?"

"Bree mentioned that you guys didn't have sex."

Yep, I knew it was coming. And it *does* piss me off.

"And that's, like, news? The fact that we dated for three months and didn't have sex?"

"Bree thought it was because of your religion."

I start to say something, and Andre holds up a hand. "I'm not passing judgment on that. I don't give a shit what you do or what you believe. But Tamsin . . . she's a free spirit. Including when it comes to sex. And I don't want to see anyone bring her down."

I'm not pissed off any more. Just confused.

"Wait a second. You think if I dated Tamsin and didn't have sex with her I'd be bringing her down?"

Andre rubs the back of his neck. "I just think the difference in your attitudes might make her feel . . . I don't know. Judged or something."

I feel my jaw tightening.

"You know what? I'm sick of people assuming that because I'm religious I'm walking around judging people."

"I didn't say—"

"I just asked if Tamsin was single. I'm not even planning to ask her out. And if I did, there's like a ninety-nine percent chance she'd say no. So you don't have to protect your friend, okay? Which, by the way, is kind of messed up. Tamsin can take care of herself. It's not very feminist of you to jump to her defense. Isn't that the patriarchy in action, or whatever?"

Andre doesn't look mad. But then he hardly ever does, even when he's tackling someone.

"What can I say? I'm from Louisiana. It's hard to take the southern gentleman out of the southern gentleman. But I live in Bracton and I've been listening to the sisterhood for two years, and they kind of have a point about—well, everything." He pauses. "Look. I know Tamsin can take care of herself. But that doesn't mean she can't get hurt, right? And I don't want to see that happen. She's in a really good place right now, and I—"

"Don't want to see her get hurt. I get it. Now please, let's get back to football. And this time I'm going to kick your ass up and down this field."

I don't, of course. But I make things as hard for Andre as I can, because it's my job to get him ready for the game on Saturday. The role of a second-string athlete isn't glamorous, but I take it seriously.

And between every play, I still can't stop thinking about Tamsin.

She's the girl who was so loud with Oscar the guy next door could hear her. She's the girl Andre calls a "free spirit" when it comes to sex.

But she also told me she's gone cold-turkey on relationships. Why isn't she dating anymore? Did something happen?

It's not just Tamsin's relationship status that has me thinking. It's also the stuff she said to me on stage and in the hallway. About abortion.

I don't believe anything because someone tells me to. I mean, there are people in my church who think homosexuality is wrong. They don't condemn the people—"love the sinner, hate the sin"—but they think the behavior is a perversion.

I think that attitude is a perversion.

There are plenty of issues where I can see two sides, but gay rights isn't one of them. One side is right and the other side is wrong. Love is love, and I believe that God smiles down on every couple with the guts to commit to each other for better or worse, richer or poorer, till death do them part.

It seems obvious to me. And so does the pro-life side of the abortion debate.

After fertilization, an embryo has its own DNA, right? Distinct from its mother and father? That means it's a separate, unique being. A *human* being. And I don't believe God would let that happen if He didn't want that embryo to become a baby.

There's a bible verse pro-life Christians quote a lot. Jeremiah 1:5.

Before I formed you in the womb I knew you,

And before you were born I consecrated you.

I know that if you're looking for a passage from scripture to support your political position, you'll probably find it. No matter what your ideology is. Even the devil can quote scripture for his purpose, and all that.

But those words are powerful to me. I do believe God knows us even before we're born. And I don't believe that we, as mere human beings, have the authority to decide which of God's consecrated children live or die.

I believe that abortion is murder.

But Tamsin said that one in four women will have an abortion in their lifetime.

One in four.

If that's true, then doesn't that mean at least one woman I know—probably more than one—has had an abortion?

Maybe I'm dumb, but it honestly never occurred to me that someone I know might have ended a pregnancy.

Maybe feminists are right about one thing. Maybe women—including pro-life women—have a perspective on abortion that's very different from a man's.

But that doesn't mean my perspective is worthless. And as I think about all that stuff Tamsin said to me, I want to argue with her about it. I want to make my case, because I believe in it.

And that's when I know I'm not dropping Experiments in Drama.

* * *

Beeker has a late class, so it's just me and Trace having dinner tonight—pizza and leftover Chinese. I make the mistake of bringing up abortion, because I was looking for someone who'd be on my side of the debate.

But I'm starting to think Trace is someone you don't want on your side. Ever.

"The whole abortion thing is such garbage," he's saying now, as pizza grease drips down his chin. He wipes it off with his sleeve. "It's just about women who can't keep their legs closed and their panties on."

I try to imagine what Tamsin would say to that.

"Thanks, man. Thanks for making me think feminists have a point about men. Especially since you slept with at least ten girls last year, and never once complained about them losing their panties."

"Well, Jesus. I'm not a fucking idiot. We used protection."

I finish my last piece of pizza and sit back on the sofa. ESPN is on TV, but even though they're talking college football I'm not paying attention.

"What if the condom broke? Or something else went wrong? What would you do if you got a girl pregnant? Would you marry her?"

Trace frowns. There's a spot of pizza grease at the corner of his mouth, and for some reason it bugs me.

"Well . . . yeah. Sure."

I pick one of the girls he slept with last year—one I know for a fact he didn't even like.

"So Mary Beth Donnelly, then? If you'd gotten her pregnant, you would've married her? Promised before God to love, honor, and cherish her? Forever?"

Trace shrugs. "I guess."

I don't know if I believe him, but I give him the benefit of the doubt.

"And what if she didn't want to marry you? What if she wanted to get an abortion? What would you do then?"

"What do you mean, what would I do?"

"Well, you don't believe in abortion, do you? So what would you do?"

Trace reaches for the last piece of pizza.

"I don't know. Try to stop her."

"How? There's no legal way. You can't get a restraining order or anything."

Trace drops the pizza slice back in the box.

"The law is never on the father's side. I'm telling you, the odds are stacked against men in this fucking country.

How disgusting is it that a man can't stop some bitch from murdering his kid?"

"Some bitch? Aren't you talking about the mother of your child?"

"Yeah, but—" He stops and glares at me. "What the hell is this, anyway? Why did you even bring this up?"

Good question. "Believe it or not, I was looking for some good pro-life arguments before my next drama class. I just went to the wrong place."

He points a greasy finger at me. "No, you didn't. Let me show you."

He pulls out his phone and starts scrolling.

"What are you doing?"

"Pulling something up on Twitter. There's a pro-choice group right here at Hart that tweets about this shit. Now they've got people all around the country on their threads. I trolled them for a while and they blocked me. So I created this new account for a college girl who 'isn't sure' about the whole abortion issue. Man, it's fun to watch them trying to indoctrinate me with their bull-shit. Here you go. This is from last night."

I take the phone he hands me, ignoring the greasy fingerprints on the screen, and look.

But what if the baby really IS a baby? Doesn't abortion stop a beating heart?

That's a tweet from what I'm guessing is Trace's sock puppet. He's named her Lisa, and her avatar is a golden retriever looking at the camera. Her profile reads, *I'm a college freshman looking for answers to life's biggest questions.*

"This is messed up, Trace."

"No, it's hilarious. Read the thread."

I scroll up to see what's above Trace's tweet. He said this started with a group here at Hart, so I look for familiar faces.

Yeah, there's a girl I've been in classes with—Mena something. And Hannah from my old dorm. And—

Tamsin.

I freeze for a second. Then I read her tweet.

What if the mother was raped? Is that a gift from God, too?

I freeze again. There's a tightness in my muscles, a spasm of nausea in my belly.

Why did Tamsin ask that question? I look at the tweet above it, which was Trace's.

Isn't every baby a gift from God?

I said something like that in the hallway after class yesterday. I said that if a couple tries not to get pregnant but does anyway, the baby must be part of God's plan.

It makes me sick that Trace used that argument as part of his fucked-up Twitter game.

I don't want to look at "Lisa's" reply to Tamsin's question, but I do.

The rape isn't a gift, but the baby is. And most rapes aren't REALLY rape. Just women changing their minds the next day.

Oh, God.

I make myself read Tamsin's reply, which is pretty restrained, all things considered.

I don't know your history or why you would say something like that, but it's not true.

And she linked to an article about campus sexual assault.

I can't look at Trace. I feel the tension in my muscles that comes before violence—the violence I channel into football. I hand his phone back and get to my feet.

"I've got to study," I say, and head for the stairs.

Trace says something as I'm leaving, but I don't answer. I need to get away so I don't punch him in the face.

After a fight turned ugly back in high school—I ended up breaking a guy's nose and fracturing his wrist—I decided I wouldn't ever use my fists in an argument again. Which means I have to turn my back on Trace right the hell now. I need to get away from the guy who could say shit like that about rape. Who could use rape in his stupid trolling campaign. Who could be flip about it, insincere about it, and a fucking douchebag about it.

Some things aren't okay, and that doesn't make me Galahad.

It makes me a human being.

CHAPTER SEVEN

Tamsin

I'm in my dorm room practicing for Experiments in Drama. Professor Washington said she wouldn't give us advance notice on scene set ups, but I know I'll be partnered with Daniel and I want to be ready.

I've spent the last twenty-four hours reading about abortion rights and thinking about abortion rights and talking with people online about abortion rights. I'm determined to win the argument once and for all, and I want to do it so convincingly that Daniel actually changes his mind.

Because in spite of him being pro-life and possibly a religious nut, I think he's a decent guy. And no decent guy should be handicapped with wrong-headed notions about the abortion debate.

"That sounds kind of judgmental," says Claire, when I start my speech to Will with that.

She, Rikki, Izzy, Mena, Julia, Will, Dyshell, and Sam are in here with me providing moral support—and in the case of Will, dramatic support. He's not an actor, but I need a stand-in for Daniel and the two of them are close in size.

Although Daniel, in my private opinion, is a little more muscular.

Will and I are standing facing each other, and the audience is sitting on the two desk chairs and on the beds—mine and Rikki's.

I'm still surprised—and really happy—that Rikki and I are sharing a room again this year. I'd been expecting her to ditch me. We've been roommates since we were freshmen, but she and Sam are practically married and I figured the two of them would get a place off-campus at some point.

But not this year, apparently.

"I'm not ready for that step yet," Rikki said. "And besides, I like living with you," she added, giving me a hug.

That's Rikki for you. Any other girl would jump at the chance to live with her boyfriend, but Rikki knows herself and she knows she isn't ready.

Like I said, she has her shit together.

So we're sharing a room again. Rikki has a whole tiger theme going on with her decorating (there's a story behind that, having to do with a sculpture Sam made of her freshman year) and her side of the room is full of tiger posters and tiger figurines and stuffed tigers.

On my side of the room, punk and goth are a major theme. Vintage vinyl album covers from the Ramones and the Clash, Rocky Horror Picture Show posters, and some of my old vampire outfits from my cosplay days.

Half of one wall is covered with peacock feather masks, voodoo dolls, and jazz posters from when I went to visit Dyshell and Andre in New Orleans. There's also some Hamilton stuff (I am a theater major, after all) and photos of friends from here at Hart and back home in San Francisco.

The only family photo is one of my grandmother.

"No pictures of your parents?" Rikki asked the first week back, the way she asked freshman and sophomore year.

"No pictures of my parents," I answered.

"You still hate them?"

"I still hate them."

And like she did freshman and sophomore year, she left it at that.

Rikki's gotten neater in the last couple years and I've gotten messier, and the room is always in a tug of war between the two states. Tonight it's fairly tidy since I asked everyone to come by. My bed, which Claire and Izzy are sitting on, is actually made for the first time in a week.

We've already chowed down on pizza and bread-sticks, and I offered everyone Mezcal as an after-dinner beverage. Izzy and Claire and I were the only takers. Then I explained how the scene would work—for the set-up, I decided to be a pro-choice activist trying to change a pro-lifer's mind—and made my opening statement to Will (aka Daniel) in which I said he was a decent guy who shouldn't be handicapped by wrongheaded notions about abortion. Now Claire, sitting cross-legged on the end of my bed, finishes her Mezcal and makes her comment.

"That sounds kind of judgmental."

"Don't you think his ideas about abortion are wrongheaded?"

"Sure. But if you start out like that, you'll put him on the defensive. You said your goal in this scene is to persuade him, right?"

"Right."

"Well, I've learned from experience that when I flat-out tell Will he's wrong about something, which he frequently is, he's not super inclined to listen to me afterward."

"That's true," Will says, grinning at her.

"Okay," I say. "No prologue calling him decent but misguided. I'll just go right into my arguments. I want you guys to tell me if they're convincing. I mean, I'm obviously preaching to the choir here, but—"

Then, suddenly, something occurs to me.

I turn away from Will and toward the rest of group. They're sitting there looking expectant.

"Uh, guys? I didn't mean to . . . that is . . ." I hesitate. "I don't want to assume that we're all pro-choice or anything. I mean, I know Rikki is, and Izzy and Mena and Julia and Dyshell and Claire, because we've talked about it, but . . ."

Sam is sitting with his arm around Rikki. "That just leaves me and Will. The guys."

"Well, yes. I don't think I've ever talked about this with either of you. If any of this offends you . . ."

Sam shakes his head. "I'm pro-choice. And even if I weren't, this wouldn't offend me."

That leaves Will. When I turn to look at him he's just standing there, shifting his weight from foot to foot and looking uncomfortable.

"I . . . don't really know what I am," he says finally.

Claire gasps. "You're not pro-*choice*?"

Her eyes are huge as she stares at her boyfriend. She looks shocked, and Will looks miserable as he stares back at her.

Shit. I only brought this up because I didn't want to make assumptions, like we all did in Experiments in Drama.

But now I realize that I *have* made assumptions. I assumed that none of my close friends—this group that's like family to me—could possibly be anti-abortion.

Will drags a hand through his reddish-brown hair. He's grown it out a little since last year, when he had to quit football after an injury.

"It's kind of a personal thing for me," Will says. "I mean . . . okay. My mom got pregnant with me when she was eighteen, and it wasn't planned. Like, big time not planned. Like, my biological father is a giant asshole. He didn't want anything to do with me or my mom when he found out."

I think of my friend in high school.

"Her parents were pretty upset too. They wanted her to have an abortion. In fact, they told her they'd kick her out of the house if she didn't." He takes a breath. "But she had me anyway. Obviously."

Claire's cheeks are pink, which happens to her when things get intense.

"I'm glad your mom had you. Obviously. But she got to make the choice that was right for her. Don't you think other women should have that same choice?"

Will doesn't look any less miserable. "Yes. Or no. I don't know. I mean, it's not like I think women should be forced to give birth or something."

"But isn't that the only other option? Either women can choose or they can't."

Mena breaks into the conversation then. She's British, and I've spent the last couple years reminding myself that her accent doesn't mean she's smarter than the rest of us—although she's premed and definitely *is* smarter than the rest of us. In some things, anyway.

"I don't know if we can think of it that way," she says. "As far as decision-making goes."

"What do you mean?" Dyshell asks.

"Decisions don't work like that. We can't think of them as the same thing both before and after they're made. If you're talking about the possibility you might not have been born, you're talking about something meaningless, because you *were* born. And if you're talking about a fertilized egg that might have become a person but didn't, that's meaningless, too. Because it didn't happen. And because of the things that did or didn't happen, peoples' lives took a certain path. But the paths that weren't taken don't have their own reality. Not in this universe, anyway."

Every so often Mena goes off on a tangent that I do not get. The one who usually does is Sam.

"Are you talking a Schrödinger's Cat kind of scenario?" Sam asks now, sounding interested.

Will sits down on the floor with his back against the closet door. I follow his cue and sit down with my back against the bookcase. I'm pretty sure neither one of us—or anyone else outside Mena and Sam—knows much about Schrödinger's Cat scenarios, but Will doesn't look as tense and bummed out as he did a minute ago, and neither does Claire.

So I figure letting Mena and Sam make the conversation a little less personal and a little more theoretical—even science nerd theoretical—isn't a bad thing for a few minutes. And anyway, it's obvious the scene between me and Will is on hold.

"Could you maybe tell the non-scientists what a Schrödinger's Cat scenario is?" I ask.

"Sure," Sam says, as Rikki gives me a why-are-you-encouraging-him look.

"Basically, you have a cat in a steel box who will die when a radioactive particle decays. But because the decay is unpredictable, you don't know when it will happen. Until the box is opened, the cat's state is completely unknown and therefore, the cat is considered to be both alive and dead at the same time until it's observed. In other words, you have to treat it as if it's doing all of the possible things—being living and dead—at the same time."

"How does that—" I start to say, but Sam just keeps going.

"If you try to make predictions about the status of the cat, you're probably going to be wrong. But if you assume it's in a combination of all of possible states that can exist, you'll be correct. Now, as soon as you actually *look* at the cat, the observer will immediately know if the cat is alive or dead and the 'superposition' of the cat—the idea that it was in both states—would collapse into either the knowledge that 'the cat is alive' or 'the cat is dead,' but not both."

My eyes are actually glazing over, but Mena's nodding like this all makes perfect sense.

"Schrödinger came up with this paradox to illustrate a point in quantum mechanics about the nature of wave particles," she says.

There's a short silence.

"Well," Claire says after a moment. "That was quite something. But I have absolutely no idea how that relates to what Will and I were talking about."

"I'm a little fuzzy on that myself," Will says.

"My point," Mena explains, "is that it doesn't make sense to look at the abortion issue on an individual level as though both possibilities—the fertilized egg becomes a child, or it doesn't—are realities. That's only true until the woman makes her choice."

Another pause.

"Yeah . . . still fuzzy," Will says.

Mena sighs. "It's just that points of decision create timelines. Forks in a person's life. And there's absolutely no way to judge the outcome based on what might have happened if you made a different choice. I mean, everyone who knows you is glad you were born, Will. But isn't it also true that a woman who had an abortion might be glad she made that choice? And that the children she goes on to have might also be glad? I mean, if she didn't have an abortion when she wasn't ready to be a mother, her life would have gone in a very different direction. She wouldn't have had the children she did later on when she was ready. And don't you think those children are glad they were born, too?"

Will and Claire speak at the same time.

"But wouldn't that—"

"How can you—"

They both stop, and Mena shrugs. "I'm just saying that the whole 'Abortion is wrong because your mom didn't abort you and aren't you happy about that' argument doesn't make much sense."

"Definitely not from a theoretical standpoint," Sam says.

"Yes. But also not from a common sense standpoint. I mean, you can't compare an event that actually did happen to all kinds of hypothetical possibilities. They're not the same, quantitatively or qualitatively. Life doesn't work that way. To put it simply, life and potential life are not the same."

"There's a thought experiment about this," Julia says suddenly.

She's been pretty quiet tonight, and we all look at her expectantly. A curl of red hair is straggling out from under the thick green headband she always wears, and she tucks it behind her ear.

"So . . . okay," she says. "Imagine you're in a fertility clinic. Or, you know, someplace where there are frozen embryos. Say a thousand, all in one container. And they're viable. I mean, they could become babies if they're implanted in a woman's uterus. I don't know if it's actually possible to fit a thousand frozen embryos in one container, but—"

"We'll assume it's possible for the sake of the thought experiment," Sam says.

"Right. So. The fire alarm goes off and flames are engulfing the building. You only have time to go into one room for a rescue. To your left is the room with the thousand frozen embryos. But in the room to your right there's a five year old child, terrified and crying for help. What do you do?"

"Rescue the child," Dyshell says immediately, and there are murmurs of agreement.

"Definitely the child," I say. And in that moment I feel a kind of clarity. The answer seems so obvious.

Julia looks at Will. "What about you? Not to put you on the spot or anything," she adds quickly.

"No, that's okay," Will says. "I'd rescue the child, too. No question."

Julia nods. "The point is that we don't really think embryos are the same as children. We think of embryos as potential life, and we don't think potential life has the same value as actual life." Her cheeks turn pink. "I thought that might tie in with Mena's thing," she adds, almost apologetically.

"It definitely does," Mena says. "It sort of navigates what I was talking about from a moral position as opposed to a quantum mechanics position, but—"

"There's another perspective on the whole abortion debate we haven't looked at yet," Izzy says abruptly.

She, like Julia, hasn't said too much tonight. Now we all look at her.

"What?" Dyshell asks.

"We could talk to someone who's actually had one."

"Well, sure," I say. "But no one here has—"

And then I stop. Because it's suddenly obvious—to all of us—that one of us *has* had an abortion.

None of us says a word. We just sort of sit there, looking at Izzy.

I finally break the silence. "I'm so sorry," I say. "If any of this has made you uncomfortable or—"

"It hasn't," she says. "I mean, it's not something I normally talk about, but you guys are my closest friends. And I was sitting here listening to everyone, and I started thinking that maybe women not talking about their abortions is one reason people feel like it's okay to talk about them in the abstract, you know? In theory instead of in reality. Because those of us who've actually gone through the experience don't talk about it."

"You shouldn't have to," Mena says fiercely. "It's your business and nobody else's."

"I know," Izzy says. "And I'm not planning to do a Facebook post or anything like that. But you guys have made me think about some stuff." She pauses. "I don't remember the procedure very well, because I was sedated. But I cried afterward. Not because I thought I murdered a baby, but because I ended a pregnancy. Potential life may not be the same as life, but it's something. And choosing to end that potential isn't nothing. It affects you. Or it affected me, anyway. I didn't make the decision lightly. It had weight.

"I've wondered *what if* sometimes, like I do about other things. But there's never been a time I wished I made a different decision."

We all just kind of sit there for a minute. Then Mena and Rikki reach out at the same time to hug her.

She puts up with it for a moment. Then, "You guys know I'm not a hugger," she says, and they let her go.

"Thanks for trusting us enough to tell us that," Will says. "Especially after what I—"

"There's nothing wrong with what you said," Izzy tells him. "You were talking about something really personal, like I was. Your mom made a choice that was right for her. I just don't think that means other people have to make the same choice. Isn't that the point of the pro-choice movement? It's a decision that should be made by a woman with the people she trusts to make it with her. I mean, there is a pro-life side to this. Only I think it's on the individual level, not the political level, if that makes any sense."

"Yeah," Will says. "That makes sense."

We're all quiet for a few seconds, looking around at each other.

"Man, this night turned intense," Claire says after a moment.

"Yeah," Sam agrees. "But we probably should have expected it when Tamsin invited us over to watch her and Will do an abortion improv. Which still hasn't happened, by the way."

"It's okay," I put in. "I'm cool. I think I've got all the material I need for tomorrow night. Daniel Bowman doesn't stand a chance."

Dyshell is sitting backward on my desk chair, her arms folded across the top and her chin resting on her forearms. Now she straightens and stares at me.

"Hold up. The guy in your class is Daniel Bowman?"

I nod.

"I know him. I mean, not well or anything, but I've met him. He's on the team with Andre. He doesn't party with those guys—Andre says he doesn't drink—but they all like him." She turns to Will. "You played with him too, right?"

Will nods. "Yeah. I didn't realize it was that Daniel we were talking about. I gotta say, out of all the guys at Hart who might have signed up for a class called Experiments in Drama, he'd be at the bottom of my list. But he's a really good guy. He's not a star athlete or anything, but he's tough as hell and always puts the team first." He hesitates. "I like him."

"Well, don't worry," I say. "I'm not planning to eviscerate him. I just want to do a good job in my scene. And thanks to you guys, I think I will."

"This has been good for me, too," Izzy says. "The truth is, I was a little worried about my own scene. I don't know who my partner will be or anything about the setup, but it's always hard when you have a personal stake. I feel better now, though. More centered."

Julia asks her a question then, something about acting, but I'm distracted by a buzz from my phone. When I pull it out of my pocket, I see a little red number one on the Twitter icon.

I haven't been on Twitter since last night. I got a mini flood of mentions then, because a bunch of us were tweeting back and forth about abortion, but that convo died down by midnight. I click on my notification tab to see what's up.

It's a direct message. I don't think I've ever gotten a direct message on Twitter before.

I click on the little envelope.

The avatar is Daniel's face. The handle is DANIEL BOWMAN, @heartofsaturdaynight.

A shiver runs through me, quick and intense. I feel cold suddenly, and then hot, like I'm getting a fever.

There's something I need to tell you. DM me back if you get this.

I look up from my phone, waiting for Izzy to finish answering Julia's question. Then I say,

"You guys think we should call it a night?"

Claire nods and gets to her feet. "I still have some work to do before bed."

Rikki says, "I hope this doesn't sound corny, but—" and then she stops.

"Finish the sentence," Dyshell puts in. "I like it when you're corny."

"It's just . . . well, this is what I always hoped college would be."

"People bearing their souls about really personal shit?" Izzy asks, grinning.

Rikki smiles back at her. "Sort of. I mean, I always wanted to have a group of friends that trusts each other enough to do that. Friends who have fun but can also talk about serious things. Things that matter. Things that aren't easy." She looks at Mena. "Even weird quantum mechanics stuff."

"We're lucky," Mena says softly, looking around at everyone.

"Yeah, we are," Will says, getting to his feet and holding his hand out to Claire. "My lady?"

I roll my eyes. "Every time you call her that, I resent not having a boyfriend. Can't you come up with an affectionate-yet-insulting nickname? Scruffy or Sneezy or Buttface?"

Will grins. "Let's go, Scruffy."

We all say our good nights and people start to head out. After a couple of minutes it's just me, Rikki, and Sam.

I hold my breath, hoping. Then Rikki says,

"I think I'm going to spend the night in Sam's room. If that's cool with you?" she asks him.

He gives her a look that probably melts her panties right off.

"That's cool with me, yeah."

Rikki gets to her feet, her cheeks pink.

"I'll see you tomorrow, Tamsin. Lunch?"

"If I'm up by then. No morning classes for me, so I'll be sleeping in."

"Okay. I'll text you."

Then the two of them are gone, and it's just me.

Me and my direct message from Daniel.

CHAPTER EIGHT

Daniel

After I leave Trace downstairs, I try to focus on classwork. It even works for a couple hours. But I can't stop thinking about what Trace said and how much it pissed me off, and eventually I call up another friend—a guy in the engineering department who also goes to our church. He's on Trace's side when it comes to a lot of issues, but he isn't a clueless asshole.

I hope he's not, anyway. Because I want a reminder that a man can be conservative without telling women how to feel about rape.

"Hey, man. What's up?" Mac says when I call.

"I have a question for you. Kind of a church thing."

"Okay."

It's not really a church thing, but I call it that because I want God to be part of this. I want to get as far away from Trace's toxic bullshit as I can, and have a conversation that comes from the better angels of our nature.

So I tell him the whole story. Then I ask,

"What should I do about Trace? I mean, the dude has issues. Should I confront him? Try to get him to talk to Father Mark? What?"

Mac is quiet for a few seconds. Then he says,

"Okay, look. Trace can be a douche, and he shouldn't be trolling people on Twitter with a fake account. But he's not wrong about those fucking feminists."

So much for the better angels of our natures.

"I mean, I think he should have the balls to talk to them direct, right? But they'd block him if he tried. You know they would. They try to pretend they're these brave warrior women or something, but they're total snowflakes. They can't stand to have a real debate. You know it's true. They need safe spaces and trigger warnings to even function. They call *us* intolerant, but *they're* the ones who think free speech only applies to people who agree with them."

I've said that kind of thing myself. Just last night, in fact. After class, I called Tamsin an intolerant liberal. I also called her an anti-religious bigot.

But before I called Mac, I went on Twitter and read her whole thread about abortion. She didn't call anybody names—not even "Lisa." She seemed to be interested in what everyone had to say, although she wasn't shy about expressing her own views.

Of course, it's hard to imagine Tamsin being shy about anything.

I think that's what appealed to me freshman year. I loved the way she walked into our dorm like she didn't give a damn about anything but being herself. She was so sexy, but she didn't flirt or try to get all the guys to want her or all the girls to be jealous of her. Maybe some guys did want her—God knows I did—and maybe some girls were jealous of her. But Tamsin didn't care one way or the other. She just cared about Oscar. That was obvious every time she looked at him.

He didn't deserve her. The truth is, I don't know if any guy deserves a girl who looks at him the way Tamsin looked at Oscar.

But he *definitely* didn't.

Okay, I'm getting distracted. Mac started it with his whole free speech riff, but now I need to get us back on track.

"All right," I say. "What's important is the Trace-is-a-douche part. That's what I've got to deal with, some way or other."

"Do you have to deal with it? I mean, can't you just let it go? I don't think he means anything by it. He'd never actually rape someone."

Because I hang with guys who make fun of feminists, I have an idea of what the feminist answer to that would be.

But never, not in a million years, would I have expected that answer to come out of my mouth.

"Even if he never rapes someone himself, he's making it easier for other guys to rape. He's contributing to rape culture."

In the silence that follows, that phrase seems to echo in the air.

"Rape culture," Mac repeats after a moment. "Rape *culture?* Are you serious right now? You sound like a social justice warrior."

Social justice warrior—SJW—is what guys like Mac and Trace call liberals. I'm no liberal, but I've never actually used that phrase as an insult. It's never made much sense to me. Social justice strikes me as a good thing.

But I'm not about to get into that. In fact, I'm starting to think calling Mac was a mistake.

So I say I have to go and end the call. Then I get up and start to pace.

I find myself looking around my room as if I'm seeing it for the first time. As Tamsin might see it if she came over.

Most of my decorating—if you can call that—is football-themed. Tamsin probably wouldn't have a problem with that. I mean, she's friends with Will and Andre, so she knows jocks.

I do have a couple of religious things. A cross-stich my mom did of the Lord's Prayer, hung up above my bookcase. And a watercolor my minister back home gave me—a picture of a waterfall with a quote by George MacDonald.

I would rather be what God chose to make me than the most glorious creature that I could think of; for to have been thought about, born in God's thought, and then made by God, is the dearest, grandest, most precious thing in all thinking.

I stop in front of that picture and read the words a couple of times. I have a book of quotes by Christian writers, and this one is in it. I copied it out and taped it to the inside of my locker during high school, when it was starting to dawn on me that I wasn't going to be class valedictorian or a star quarterback . . . or the best at anything, really. I told Father Warren about that realization and how the George MacDonald quote helped me, and he gave me this picture for graduation.

The painting of the waterfall isn't that great. The frame is kind of ugly. But at least a year after I talked to him about that quote, my minister remembered it and bought that picture for me.

A small kindness. The kind of thing Father Warren does so often he probably doesn't even think about it. But it means a lot to the people on the receiving end.

There's another quote by George MacDonald that I like.

There are thousands willing to do great things for one willing to do a small thing.

I like that one because it's true. People are always willing to do the big stuff—the stuff that gets you attention. But people forget to do the little things. The day to day things. Just trying to be strong and honest and kind and brave when it doesn't seem to matter or when no one's looking.

I go over to my bed and lie down, my arms folded behind my head. As I stare up at the ceiling I'm thinking, what small thing can I do right now to make things better?

To be honest, I can't think of anything that will make the Trace situation better. Not right now, anyway. Maybe I need to sleep on that one.

But there's something else I can do. I can tell Tamsin that the "Lisa" who's been popping into her online discussions is a fake account.

I don't have her phone number. But when I pull up her profile on Twitter, I see that her DMs are open.

There's something I need to tell you. DM me back if you get this.

Now I'm just here on my bed, waiting. Which is stupid, because it's midnight and Tamsin's probably asleep. Even if she's awake, she hasn't been on Twitter since last night. Why would she even notice I DMed her?

Refresh. Refresh.

Man, I'm an idiot.

Refresh.

And then . . .

Ding.

I sit straight up in bed, staring at my phone. It made the notification sound, and there's also a little red number one on the envelope icon on the bottom right corner of my Twitter screen.

I click on it.

What?

That's all.

I hesitate. There's no character limit in DMs, so I can say whatever I want.

You've been talking with someone named Lisa on Twitter. The golden retriever avatar. She's actually my asshole housemate trolling pro-choice girls from Hart. Just block him. Tell your followers to block him too.

Maybe a minute goes by. Then:

Wow. Okay, I will. Thanks for telling me. But I gotta say, in case you haven't noticed . . . you seem to be friends with a lot of assholes. It's none of my business, but I thought I'd point it out.

There's Shane, who called her a skank. And Trace, who told her rape is just a girl changing her mind the next day.

I type, *I've got some friends who aren't assholes,* and erase it.

Then I type, *Yeah, maybe,* and erase that, too.

I stare down at my phone for a few seconds. Then I type,

Sorry.

Her reply comes a minute later.

It's none of my business, like I said. But YOU'RE not an asshole.

My phone is cradled in my hand, and I move my thumb over Tamsin's message on the screen. Then I type,

Thanks.

It's a pretty lame reply, but sometimes a lame reply is all you've got.

I just call em like I see em. So are you coming to class tomorrow? Or were all the liberals too much for you? Do you need a safe space, snowflake?

I grin.

I'll be there. What about you?

I wouldn't miss it. I'm going to wipe up the floor with you, by the way.

Doubtful. See you tomorrow, Tamsin.

See you tomorrow, Daniel.

It's the first time she's called me by my name. And even though she did it in a Twitter DM, I hear it in her voice. That low, sexy, smoky voice I heard for the first time freshman year, when the prettiest girl I ever saw came to my dorm to see her boyfriend.

CHAPTER NINE

Daniel

After football practice and before Experiments in Drama, I go to church.

I call ahead to see if the minister has any free time that afternoon. His secretary makes an appointment for me, and I show up at the rectory around five o'clock.

I feel a lot better after I talk to Father Mark. I don't know him as well as I know Father Warren back home, but he's a good man. I tell him the story behind my visit—what we're doing in Experiments in Drama, and my chance to do a sort of pro-life ministry.

It's a huge relief to hear pro-life arguments made by someone not an asshole. As I eat dinner later and head to class, I feel good. Father Mark's words resonated with me, and I think I can make them resonate for other people, too.

Father Mark warned me against using religion as a weapon, and I have no plans to do that. But I'm going to make my case, and there's no way Tamsin—or anyone else—can make one that's any stronger.

When I walk into the theater, Tamsin is already there. She's talking to her friend Izzy and a guy whose name I can't remember.

In the moments before she notices me in the doorway, I have a chance to look at her.

Okay, stare at her.

Damn, she's beautiful.

I'm glad the lights are dim in here, because I'm worried about what my face might be showing. The fact is, I'm really glad to see Tamsin again, and I'm pretty sure my expression isn't hiding that fact.

She used to dye her hair jet black. It's lighter now, and I think the shade is her natural one. It's still really dark, almost black, and it's long and wavy and silky-looking. She's wearing a red cotton shirt, and her hair looks amazing against it.

Her makeup is dramatic. Maybe not as much as freshman year, but she still wears more than most of the girls I know.

I used to think I didn't like that. I used to think au naturel was the way to go. But I love the way Tamsin uses makeup. Not to hide flaws or anything, but almost like a painter would use a canvas: for sheer love of decoration.

It's dramatic around her eyes especially. She does this kind of intense, smoky eye shadow thing, with either the best mascara money can buy or the longest natural eyelashes any girl ever had.

It makes her gray eyes look huge.

Her lips are less intense. Pale pink, full and soft. But whatever she does to them makes them so kissable I don't know how any guy near her can think of anything else.

God knows I can't.

But then Professor Washington comes in and Tamsin looks up, and I go to an empty seat in the front row.

I expect the professor to go right into our scenes, and I'm ready. I'm armed with everything Father Mark and I talked about, and I'm going to change Tamsin's mind if it's the last thing I do.

First, though, the professor tells us all to come up on stage and make a circle. After telling us to call her Joan, she has us all go around and give our names and the reasons we wanted to take this class.

Tamsin starts us off. "My name is Tamsin Shay, and I'm a theater major. I know a lot of people who've taken Experiments in Drama, and they all rave about it. My friend Julie said it helped her remember why she wanted to act in the first place. She said you teach a strategy of radical honesty, and it helped her be more authentic in everything she was doing."

She hesitates. "A part of me was really drawn to that phrase—radical honesty. Another part of me was scared by it if I'm being . . . well, honest."

She's wearing jeans with her red shirt, and now she sticks her hands in her pockets. "Anyway, I'm excited to take this class. And a little scared, too."

We're going clockwise, which means they'll get to me after five people. I look at Izzy when she's talking, and then at Charlie (that's the guy whose name I couldn't remember), and at the three people who come after that. But I don't really hear them. I'm thinking about Tamsin, and what she said.

Radical honesty.

When Professor Washington—Joan—nods at me, I start talking. But I don't say what I'd planned to say.

"My name is Daniel Bowman. I'm an engineering major. I signed up for this class because I need one more arts credit before I graduate, and I wanted to get it over with before next year. There were five classes that fit into my schedule, and I thought this one would have the least amount of work." I pause. "But that's not the only reason, if I'm being honest." I pause again. "I was in a play back in junior high. And I, uh, liked it. So here I am," I finish awkwardly.

There's a short silence. My face feels hot. I'm not looking at anyone in particular, because I don't want to meet anyone's eyes.

Then Professor Wa—Joan, I mean—says,

"Thanks, Daniel. No matter the reason you're here, we're glad that you are. All right, Kelly, you're next."

Kelly starts to talk, and as she does, I glance across the circle at Tamsin.

She's looking right at me, and one corner of that soft pink mouth is lifted in a smile.

I try to read her expression. Surprised? Friendly? Warm? Something like that.

Anyway, I like it.

"All right, everyone, let's get started with our scenes. Tamsin and Daniel, stay on stage. The rest of us will sit in the audience."

A minute later, Tamsin and I are facing each other.

"Are you ready for this?" I ask softly.

"I was born ready."

She's smiling, and so am I. I replay my conversation with Father Mark, marshaling my arguments in my head. I'm not going to be caught flat-footed no matter what Tamsin throws at me.

Joan is sitting in the middle of the front row. "Okay, you two, here's the set up. Tamsin, you're a pro-life activist. Daniel, you're a doctor who provides abortions. Okay, go."

I blink. Tamsin blinks. For a moment we just stare at each other.

Then we both turn toward Joan and start talking at the same time.

"How are we supposed to—"

"I thought this scene was—"

Joan holds up a hand. "This is improv, cats and kittens. You're supposed to get out of your comfort zones. Remember?"

Tamsin looks frustrated. "But I thought this class was about radical honesty, too. How am I supposed to be radically honest and pretend to be pro-life at the same time?"

Joan grins at her. "This is an acting class. It's all about pretending. Walking in someone else's shoes, right? Can you find the radical honesty in another person's reality? That's the challenge here."

I open my mouth to speak, but Joan holds up her hand again. "That's enough complaining. Let me remind you that this is improv and you don't get time to plan. Be in the moment. Your costume is the body and mind of another person. Ready, set, *go*!"

I've been thinking about this moment for the last two days. I've been picturing standing here on stage just like this, facing Tamsin. I practiced all my arguments in favor of life. I was *ready*, damn it! And now all that preparation is out the window.

I have no idea what's going to happen next.

CHAPTER TEN

Tamsin

I have no idea what's going to happen next.

What am I supposed to do now? After last night, I felt like I had a sword to carry into this battle that no one could stand against. I felt strong and centered in my beliefs and in myself.

How can I feel centered in someone *else's* beliefs?

That's literally what acting is.

The voice inside my head sounds like Joan's, and I resent it.

But she's not wrong. So, okay. It's obvious when I look at Daniel that he's just as flummoxed as I am. And he doesn't have my experience in theater, so it's up to me to make this scene work.

I take a deep breath.

"I know you probably want to get home to your family. But I also know what you spent your day doing, Doctor, and I want to talk to you about it."

Daniel looks groggy but game. Props to him for not giving up on the spot.

"Are you planning to gun me down like you did George Tiller?"

George Tiller was the doctor shot by an anti-abortion extremist in a Kansas church.

Not bad, Daniel. Not bad at all.

"I didn't shoot George Tiller," I say. "I would never do something like that. I believe every life is sacred. That's why I'm here. That's why I want to talk to you."

Daniel looks at his wrist as though at a watch.

"It's been a long day. I'll give you two minutes."

I clear my throat. "Every life is sacred," I say.

I'm repeating myself. Bad theater.

I try again. "As a doctor, didn't you take an oath to do no harm? Isn't it your job to protect life, not to take it?"

Better.

"If you think that's somehow black and white, you don't know anything about being a doctor."

Daniel actually seems to be settling into this role. His arms are folded, he's frowning, and he looks like he's working hard to stay patient. He also looks a little supercilious, which is exactly how most doctors I've met look.

It suddenly occurs to me that he might do better in this scene than me.

Except, no way. I will *not* let that happen. Of the two people on stage right now, only one of them is an acting major.

"So you're saying that in your opinion, it's perfectly okay to kill babies?"

"A fetus isn't a baby."

"Oh, really? What about late term partial birth abortion? What about abortion after the fetus is viable? Isn't that a baby?"

Daniel is doing a really good job of looking down his nose at me. Of course it helps that his nose is like a foot above mine.

"First of all, partial birth abortion is illegal, so that's a straw man argument."

I didn't realize Daniel actually knew that.

"Second of all, do you know how many abortions are done late term, after the fetus is viable?"

Of course I do. But would my character?

"Too many," I say.

"1.2%. And by the way, I'm not one of the doctors who performs that type of procedure, so if you want to fight with me about that it'll be theoretical."

Damn.

"But," he continues, "if we're going to talk about the most extreme arguments in this debate, what about the other side?"

"The other side?"

"Rape, incest, and the life of the mother. Do you believe abortion should be illegal in those cases? Would you force a victim of rape to carry a pregnancy to term against her will? Would you rather see a woman die than have an abortion, if her life is in danger?"

"Yes," I say, thinking that my character would.

But that sounds too extreme. It's not believable. If I'm taking this seriously, I have to make it believable.

"I mean, no. If the woman's life is actively in danger, I think abortion is acceptable. It's a terrible choice and a tragedy, but it should be legal."

"What about women who've been raped? Do you want to see them forced to give birth?"

I remember Daniel's DM last night, about his asshole housemate trolling me on Twitter. And it's the asshole housemate I channel right now.

"Rape is a terrible thing. But you don't have the right to kill a baby just because its life began in a terrible way. And besides," I say, "we all know the rape argument is just an excuse for abortion on demand. If we make abortion illegal except in cases of rape, incest, and the life of the mother, then any woman with an unwanted pregnancy could just claim she was raped."

I'm kind of on a roll now. A roll of horribleness.

"If you spent any time on a college campus, you'd know how bogus all these rape charges are. The truth is, girls like to have sex. They just don't always like the consequences. And all that consent garbage goes against human nature, anyway. The male sex drive is all about dominance and being alpha. If you try to get men to follow all these consent rules you'll kill their natural sexual urges, and then—"

"Bullshit."

I stop, staring at Daniel with my mouth open. "What?"

"I said, bullshit. Rape isn't about sex. It's about power."

He said that like he believed it. Is this acting, or real life?

"What are you—"

"Rape is one person using their power to take away someone else's. It's not a sex act. It's an act of violence. So you're saying that a woman who's been the victim of violence, who's had control of her own body taken away from her by force, should have that control taken away again. You're saying she should be forced to give birth against her will, after she was forced to become pregnant against her will. You're saying that what she wants doesn't matter. You're saying that *she* doesn't matter." Daniel takes a deep breath. "Well, I'm saying she *does* matter. And I'm going to fight like hell to make sure people like you don't take away her rights."

I can't think of a single thing to say after that.

And then, like during last class, the room bursts into applause.

"End scene," Joan says. "Daniel, I wish I'd seen you in your junior high school play. Okay, who's next? Charlie, who's your partner?"

I don't hear a word of Charlie's scene, or any of the scenes that come after. Daniel is all I can think about.

He's one hell of an actor. Or could that passion have been real?

He's sitting in the front row, a few seats over from Joan. He keeps his eyes dutifully on the action happening on stage. He doesn't turn around once, even though I'm sitting just two rows behind him and a little to the left.

I decide to talk to him after class. He stays behind to ask Joan something, and I leave with everyone else. But then, like Daniel did last time, I wait in the shadows under the stairwell.

I count the students leaving. There are sixteen of us altogether. Thirteen, fourteen, fifteen. Just Joan and Daniel left in there now. Then the door opens and they come out, still talking.

I step in front of them. "Sorry to interrupt, but . . . could I talk to you for a second?" I ask Daniel.

Joan smiles. "I'll leave you to it," she says. "Good work today, you two. See you next time." Then she leaves, her shoes echoing on the linoleum floor.

Neither of us says anything until the exit door closes behind her.

Then:

"What's up?" Daniel asks. His expression is curious, and there's a hint of a smile at one corner of his mouth.

I slide my hands into the pockets of my jeans. "I just wanted to know if you meant it. What you said in our scene."

He doesn't pretend not to know what I'm talking about, which I appreciate.

"About rape? Yeah, I meant it. I'm not *that* good an actor."

I take a step closer to him. It's dead quiet in this hallway, and one of the fluorescent bulbs above us is out. One side of Daniel's face is lit and the other is in shadow.

"Can I ask you a personal question?"

He shrugs. "This whole damn class is like a personal question. What's one more?"

"Do you know someone who was raped?"

I hold my breath waiting for the answer. I'm not sure I should have asked it, but it's too late to take it back now.

The lighting makes it hard to read his expression. I look into his eyes—they're dark blue, almost navy—and I can't tell what he's thinking, or if he's angry with me.

With half his face in shadow he looks almost . . . I don't know, dangerous. Which is ridiculous, because

Daniel Bowman is probably the least dangerous guy I've ever met. Dyshell said he doesn't even drink.

On the other hand, he is a football player. If there's one thing I've learned from Andre and Will, it's that anybody willing to get pounded on that field day in and day out is tough. And capable of violence, even if they only ever express it through the game.

I can't read Daniel's expression, but something about him right now—the way he's holding himself, maybe—makes me very aware that he's capable of violence.

Maybe he's thinking of the girl he knows who was raped.

"No," he says, just as I'm reminding myself that he hasn't answered my question yet. "Not raped."

Something tells me that's far from the whole story. But I can't bring myself to ask anything else.

"I shouldn't have brought it up. I'm sorry. It's just that in our scene, you . . ."

"What?" he asks after a moment.

"You were kind of . . . intense. In a good way," I add. "I mean, you did a great job."

The corner of his mouth goes up again.

"You only think that because I was taking your side of the argument."

"But you said you agreed with part of my argument. At least . . . maybe I'm assuming too much. If you got your way and abortion was banned, would you want to see exceptions for rape, incest, and the life of the mother?"

"Yeah."

I guess that's something.

Arguments rise up inside me about the other reasons women choose abortion—women like Izzy and my friend from high school. But the truth is, I wish we could talk about something else for a while.

We could if we were friends. We could talk about lots of things.

But we're not friends. And it doesn't seem likely that we ever will be.

"Hey, Tamsin?"

He's going to tell me he has to go now.

"I know, it's getting late. I'll see you next—"

"I'm going to take you out on a date."

I blink.

"I'm sorry, what?"

That quirk at the corner of his mouth has turned into a full-on grin, and it's sexy as fuck.

"You heard me."

"But that's—I don't—why would you—"

I can't think how to finish any of the sentences I started, so I stop talking.

It seems so unlikely that Daniel Bowman would want to take me on a date that for a second, I wonder if he's actually making fun of me.

But a joke like that would be mean, and Daniel isn't mean.

"I don't understand," I say finally.

Daniel drops his backpack on the floor and leans back against the stairwell.

"It's not that complicated," he says, sounding like he's enjoying himself. "I'm going to take you on a date. Have you ever been on one?"

Okay, that's insulting. "What are you talking about? You lived in Oscar's dorm, didn't you? You saw us together all the time."

"Yeah, I did. That's why I'm asking. Oscar didn't strike me as the kind of guy who would take a girl on a date."

Now I see what he's driving at.

"You're talking about picking a girl up at her place, giving her flowers or whatever, and taking her out to dinner and a movie?"

Damn that grin.

"Now you've got it. Have you ever been on one of those?"

"It's not 1950, so no. For one thing, I like to pay my own way. I never let a guy pay for me. Not even a movie ticket."

"See, now, this is one of the things feminism gets wrong. The guy should pay on a date. Especially the first one."

I fold my arms. "Money is power. Financial independence is power. I choose not to give a guy the illusion that he has power over me."

He looks at me for a moment, his head cocked to the side. Then he shakes his head slowly.

"When two people are into each other, they take turns having power. But that's not why a guy pays on a date. Or at least, it's not why I pay."

That short beard of his makes me want to run a hand along the line of his jaw.

"Okay, I'll bite. Why do you pay?"

"Because on a date, a guy is auditioning for the role of someone who wants to dote on you. And because it's romantic."

I feel hot and then cold. What is happening here? What is he saying? Is he . . . does he . . .

"You want to dote on me?" I blurt.

He flashes that grin again.

"That would freak you out, wouldn't it? So I won't say it. I'll just say I think it would be fun to take you on a date. To show you how a real man does it."

A real man.

I feel like I'm struggling to keep up at this point, but I take another shot at it.

"You want to take me on a date not because you're into me, but as a kind of . . . demonstration?"

He shrugs. "Sure, let's call it that. A show-you-how-it's-done kind of thing. I had to watch Oscar screw up his time with you for an entire year, and I want you to know that some guys aren't assholes. That some guys are actually worth your trouble."

My arms are still folded, and they feel like my only protection from this weird melting feeling inside me, right behind my breastbone.

"You want to take me on a date on behalf of the male gender as a whole? To prove that some of you are decent?"

"Yeah."

"But not because you're into me."

It's the second time I've used that phrase, and I feel my cheeks heating up.

He shakes his head.

It occurs to me then that I asked the question wrong. I should have just said, *Are you into me?* Because the way I put it leaves room for the interpretation that while his *primary* reason for taking me on a date isn't that he's into me, he could, in fact, be into me.

But there is no way on God's green earth I'm going to attempt to clarify this point. Because believe it or not, I actually do have some pride.

"But while we're on the subject, do you know what I figured out today?" he asks.

"What?"

He takes a step closer. Even though he's not touching me, goose bumps sweep across my skin. Then he bends his head, bringing his mouth to within an inch of my ear.

"*You're* into *me*."

Now it's not just my face that's hot. It's my whole body, from my head right down to my toes.

I take a step back, my legs shaky.

"You're out of your mind," I say automatically—even though it's a lie.

He's better lit now, and those navy blue eyes are impossible to look away from.

"You were staring at me all during class."

I'm amazed I don't break into a flop sweat.

"That's—that's just because—" I swallow. "I was thinking about our scene. And anyway, how the hell do you know where I was looking? Do you have eyes in the back of your head or something?"

"I didn't know," he says, his expression smug. "It was just a guess."

Well, shit.

I wish I knew how to wipe that grin off his face. But there's no question he won this round.

I try to get the conversation back on point.

"Look, Bowman. I don't go on dates as social experiments or whatever."

"That's not why you'll go. You'll go because you're into me."

"I'm not—"

"I'll pick you up Saturday night at seven. We'll go out to dinner, but it'll be a casual place. You can wear whatever you want."

"I won't—"

"Yeah, you will."

I huff out an annoyed breath. "What makes you think I'll go on this date with you?"

"I don't know for sure," he says. "It's another guess. But I'll be right again, because you're into me."

He still hasn't said whether *he's* into *me*. I want to ask him, because the power dynamic is totally screwed up right now and I want him to feel as off balance as I do.

But I can't ask him. Obviously. I mean, what if he says no?

What if he says yes?

And that's when I realize I don't know which answer would be scarier.

All I can do is stare at him, feeling like I'm not wearing enough clothes. But it's not my skin that's exposed.

"What about after the date?" I ask suddenly.

"What do you mean?"

"What are you expecting?"

I'm not sure why I'm asking this. Is it my way of asking if he's into me without asking if he's into me?

"Nothing," he says. "In fact, that's the first ground rule for Saturday night. No fooling around. Not even kissing."

I feel myself relax a little, which is confusing. I *am* actually into this guy, and I'm a girl with a healthy sex drive. So why should I feel relieved about the no-fooling-around thing?

Not that I've even agreed to go on the date, of course.

"What's the second ground rule?"

"We don't talk about abortion. Or religion. Or politics."

I start to smile. "That sounds good." I pause. "But I haven't said yes yet."

"I know. But you will."

He looks at something over my shoulder, and I turn to see Izzy and Charlie coming down the hallway.

"Your friends are looking for you," Daniel says. "I'll see you Saturday night, Tamsin."

Then he picks up his backpack and walks away.

CHAPTER ELEVEN

Daniel

This is the first night of the new school year that I've really felt autumn coming.

Thank God for that. My heart is pounding and my face is hot, and I need that hint of cool in the air. I walk fast across the quad, not even sure where I'm going, but knowing I need to get away from Tamsin.

What the hell did I just do?

It was that damn class. That damn radical honesty thing. It pulled all those words out of me onstage, and I felt naked afterward. And then, still naked, I met Tamsin outside the theater door.

Shit, shit, shit.

Here's some advice. If you're into a girl but you shouldn't be a couple, don't take an acting class with her. Because it'll leave you raw, with nothing between you and how much you want her, and you'll do something stupid like ask her out on a date.

That stupid fucking scene. The stupid fucking things I said. I mean yeah, they were true, but they ripped open a wound so rotten and festering I was terrified everyone in that theater had seen it.

Tamsin had.

Do you know someone who was raped?

No, I said. *Not raped.*

Talk about half truths. Talk about lying by omission.

So much for radical honesty.

But I thank God for that, too. I thank God I didn't blurt out the truth to the girl I have a crush on.

It was me. But I wasn't raped. I was only molested.

I've crossed the quad now, and the library is in front of me. There's a little garden around back that no one ever goes into, and that's where I head.

I come to the iron fence and the brick path leading into the garden. The path winds around a little and then circles a big maple tree.

There's a stone bench on the far side. I sit down, the trunk at my back and the tree branches above my head.

The garden is lit by the glow of the library windows. This is one of the oldest buildings on campus and the windows are tall and arched, kind of gothic looking. Light spills through them onto the ivy and trees and bushes out here.

Inside that building are hundreds of students reading, writing, and studying. Normal people doing normal things.

I've never felt less like one of them.

I've never told anyone about what my neighbor did to me eight years ago. I never will. I didn't even tell Father Warren, because he'd want me to tell my mother.

The last thing she needs is to feel guilty because she didn't protect me or help me or whatever. It's just her, my little sister, and me, and that's enough of a burden for a single mom.

It's been eight years since it happened, and I don't think about it much anymore. Sometimes weeks will go by and I don't think about it once. That's one of the advantages of not dating, to be honest. Because as much as I love kissing and fooling around, what happened when I was twelve years old screwed me up when it comes to sex.

Which makes it pretty damn hard to have a normal relationship.

It took me a while to even be able to masturbate. I felt disconnected from my own body for a long time. I do plenty of that now, at least. But no girl has ever made me come.

I fantasize about it. There was a stretch freshman year when I fantasized about Tamsin every damn night. But when I'm actually with a girl, even if I'm totally into things, I freeze up if she tries to go down on me or even touch me.

I've figured out ways to avoid that happening. The secret is being so good at making a girl come that she's perfectly happy to stick with that.

It helps that I love going down on girls. And a good kissing session can go on for hours.

I don't have any issues with our bodies touching—the grinding that happens when you're making out. It's just when a girl goes to unzip my pants that I get messed up.

I always figured I'd get over it someday. I hope I do. But it's not going to happen with Tamsin.

Tamsin is totally comfortable with her body, with sex, with herself. There's no way she'd be happy just to kiss a guy she's dating, or even just to let him go down on her. And how would I explain not wanting to go further?

I can't lie and say it's about religion, because it isn't. Some people in my church want to wait until they're married, and that's fine—but I don't have a problem with premarital sex.

It's not that I don't want to do it. It's that I can't do it. And there is no way, absolutely no fucking way, that I'm going to let Tamsin Shay see exactly how screwed up I am. I've lusted after this girl since the first time I saw her, and I couldn't stand for her to find out that part of me is broken.

Maybe it's old-fashioned. Maybe it's bullshit. But if you're going to be with a girl like Tamsin, a girl who's smart and funny and challenging and sexy, I think you should be whole. I think you should have something to offer her.

I slide down on the bench a little, resting on my tailbone. The cool breeze feels good and my heart rate has settled down. It's time to stop freaking out and put things in perspective.

Okay, so I'm not whole. And if we were talking about a relationship, then yeah, I wouldn't have much to offer Tamsin.

But I didn't say anything about a relationship. I didn't ask her to be my girlfriend. I didn't even admit I'm into her, although she probably figured that much out.

What I did was ask her on a date. And whatever part of my brain is in charge of self-preservation kicked in, because I told her I just want to show her what a date should be like. How a real man should treat her.

As opposed to, say, an asshole like Oscar.

So, fine. I can stick with that. No kissing, I said. No fooling around. Just a good old-fashioned date.

All during freshman year I saw Tamsin do little things for Oscar—bake cookies for him and get coffee for him and rub his shoulders and help him study for tests—while he hardly ever did anything for her.

That's fucked up. And if I can stay focused on that—on treating Tamsin the way she deserves to be treated—then I'll be okay.

It's just one night, after all. One date. And after that, things will go back to normal between Tamsin and me. We'll have zero in common, spar in class, and disagree about pretty much everything.

But maybe Tamsin's next relationship will be with the kind of guy she deserves. And if I can show her what that looks like, then the torture of a romantic night with a girl I'll never be with will be worth it.

CHAPTER TWELVE

Tamsin

"How do I look?"

I haven't been this nervous to go out with a guy in years. I spent the last two days thinking about what to wear, and I finally settled on the white blouse and gray skirt I wore to my cousin's wedding last summer. My makeup is minimal, my hair is up, and I'm wearing my low-heeled Mary-Janes.

Rikki looks up from her book and studies me for a long moment.

"Well?" I ask finally. "What's the verdict? How do I look?"

"Like you're about to knock on a stranger's door to talk about the miracle of God's love. If that's what you're going for, well done."

I turn to look in the mirror. Is she right?

Maybe. I mean, I don't think I've gone full-fledged Jehovah's Witness or anything, but it occurs to me that if I were going on a job interview, this is the outfit I'd wear.

Well, that's depressing. I thought I did such a good job.

"Shit," I mutter. "Now what? I have literally no idea what to wear on this damn date."

"May I offer some advice?"

I sigh and turn back to Rikki. "Sure, why not. My night can't get any worse."

She puts her book down on the bed and sits up straight.

"Okay, look. This guy is into *you,* Tamsin. Not this other weird girl I've never met. What's the first album on your Annie Lennox playlist?

Rikki has been doing this thing lately where she communicates with me via song and album titles, which is kind of adorable when you consider that she hardly knew anything about music until I took her under my wing.

"Be Yourself Tonight."

"There you go. My advice in a nutshell. I mean, you'd never let someone else slut shame you, right?"

"Of course not."

"Well, dressing like this seems like a passive aggressive way of slut-shaming yourself. So unless this is a genuine fashion choice, don't fucking do it."

Rikki hardly ever swears. I always pay attention when she does.

"What am I supposed to wear, then?"

"Whatever makes you happy." Rikki waves a hand at me. "Does that outfit make you happy?"

I look down at myself. "No."

"Okay, then. Wear something that does."

The advice Rikki just gave me is the advice I give other women when they go out. Wear what makes you happy, because being comfortable with yourself is always the sexiest accessory.

How could I have forgotten that? Is there something about Daniel that made me forget it?

If we were going on a real date, this would be a bad sign. I decided last year I'd rather be single than in a relationship that makes me feel shitty about myself.

Now here I am, ready to dress like someone else in the hopes of pleasing some guy.

"Thanks," I say to Rikki.

"No problem," she says, going back to her book.

Ten minutes later I ask her again.

"How do I look now?"

She looks up, studies me for a second, and then grins.

"Like a million bucks. Daniel's not going to know what hit him."

"It's not a real date," I remind her.

"Sure, go with that."

"It's not!"

"Uh huh."

Oh, forget it. I turn away from Rikki and check myself in the mirror.

I'm wearing a black cotton mini skirt and four inch heels. I dressed it down with a T-shirt—black with a pink glitter heart—and dressed it up with the real diamond earrings my grandmother gave me. I'm wearing my favorite blood-red lipstick, dark gray eye shadow, and black liquid eyeliner.

When I realize I'm smiling at my reflection, I know I've made the right choice.

I realize something else, too. I want to make Daniel eat his words.

No kissing and fooling around, he said.

Well, I can handle that if I have to. I've gone without sex for a year. But by the end of the night, I want Daniel hanging on by a thread to his own ground rules.

Or better yet, breaking them.

I check the time, and it's 6:53. Seven minutes to wait.

"Should I go down to the common room or stay here?"

Rikki looks up from her book again.

"He said he was picking you up, right?"

"Yes. But what does that mean?"

"Well, you described this guy as the old-fashioned type. So I'd say whatever would be the least trouble for you and the most trouble for him."

"So I should stay here."

"That's what I'd do."

I sit down on the edge of my bed and wait.

6:54 and counting.

I have butterflies in my stomach. Although, to be honest, that's a sweet euphemism for what's actually happening. The truth is, I'm feeling nauseous.

That can't be good.

"What can't be good?" Rikki asks, and I realize I spoke out loud.

"I'm nervous. Sick to my stomach. How am I suppose to charm the pants off Daniel Bowman if I'm nervous and sick to my stomach?"

Rikki closes her book. "You've got it backward. If this is an old-fashioned date, it's *his* job to charm *you.* Your job is just to sit back, relax, and let him do all the work."

I think about that for a minute. And then, slowly, it dawns on me that what Rikki's describing would be kind of . . . nice.

It would be nice not to think about whether a guy likes my outfit, or thinks I'm funny or pretty or sexy, or if he likes the movie or restaurant I picked out. It would be nice to be doted on.

A little weird, but nice.

I start to relax a little. It's exactly seven o'clock. I'm starting to wonder if I should go downstairs after all when there's a knock on the door.

And then, just like that, my nerves come back.

I jump to my feet and cross the room. When I open the door, Daniel's standing in the hallway with a smile on his face and a bouquet of daisies in his hand.

He looks amazing. He's wearing a dark red shirt and khaki pants. His hair is tousled in that sexy way some guys can pull off so well, and the clippers he used to trim his beard were obviously set to sexy as fuck.

"Hi," he says, and when the sound of his voice makes the back of my neck prickle, it occurs to me I might be in some trouble here.

"Hi," I say, feeling shy and stupid and ridiculous and awkward.

I try to remember what Rikki said about *him* needing to charm *me*.

His eyes travel down to the tips of my toes—blood red like my lips—and back up to my face.

"You look incredible," he says, and I actually blush.

I mean, my God. Rikki and Claire blush. Not me.

"Tamsin," Rikki says behind me. "Aren't you going to introduce me to your young man?"

I roll my eyes, but it's obvious from his grin that Daniel thinks she's pretty funny.

Oh well, what the hell. If we're doing old-fashioned why not *really* do it, right?

"Rikki Eisendrath, allow me to present Daniel Bowman. Daniel, this is my roommate, Rikki."

Daniel hands me the bouquet of daisies—snowy white against green leaves—and goes over to shake Rikki's hand.

"It's a pleasure to meet you," he says.

She smiles, and I can tell she likes him.

"The pleasure is all mine. I've lifted Tamsin's curfew for this occasion, so you kids have fun." She nods at my bouquet. "I'll put those in water for you."

On an impulse, I pull out one daisy. I snap off all but a few inches of the stem and slide it behind my ear.

Then I hand the bouquet to Rikki and turn back to Daniel.

He's looking around the room, and I'm very glad I tidied up my half earlier today.

"This looks like you," he says. "I like it."

In spite of my resolution not to care what he likes or doesn't like about me, I feel warmed by the compliment.

"Thanks," I say. "Should we go?"

He nods and offers me his arm, which is almost too old-fashioned. But I take it, figuring he's setting the tone for the evening, and I discover that a side benefit of being squired around like a Victorian maiden is getting to feel up Daniel's bicep.

It's quite impressive.

Which reminds me: taking me on a date wasn't the only thing on Daniel's agenda today.

"I'm sorry you guys lost the game," I tell him as we go down the stairs. "It was pretty close, though. 24-21, right?"

He nods. "Did you actually watch us play? Andre says you're not much of a football fan, though he gives you props for trying."

He's talked to Andre about me?

"I admit I didn't see the whole thing. I caught the last quarter, though."

"That's too bad. You missed five minutes during the first half when I was actually on the field."

I glance up at him. He doesn't sound bitter or anything, which reminds me of what Will said about him.

"Do you mind if I ask you a personal question?"

We're downstairs now, at the front door. Daniel holds it open for me.

"More personal than the last question you asked me?"

I walk through and wait for him to follow, and then he offers me his arm again.

"No, not that personal," I say as we head away from campus and toward downtown. "I was just wondering if you mind not being a starter on the team."

It's the weekend, which means we're not the only students heading off campus for a night out. The sidewalk is crowded and Daniel pulls me closer to him. The air isn't cold but it's crisp, and the warmth from his body feels good.

Really good.

My knees are a little shaky, and I'm starting to wonder if the four-inch heels were a good idea. On the plus side, though, the height difference between us has been cut by a third.

We're at the perfect kissing distance, in fact. Although if Daniel has his way, kissing won't be a thing tonight.

"I'm cool with not being a starter," he says. "I made my peace with that a while ago. I mean, I still have hopes of getting more playing time—especially next year, when I'll be a senior. But not everyone can be first string, right? You need reliable backup players, too. You can't have a team without them."

There's something so . . . I don't know, generous about that statement. Especially when I contrast it with my own attitude about being a backup player.

I'm quiet for a moment, thinking about that, and when we stop at a crosswalk Daniel nudges me gently.

"What is it?"

"Nothing," I say. "I mean, I was just remembering how I complained about being an understudy last year or being cast in minor roles. You're a lot more humble than I am. I've always got my eye out for a spotlight, and if I see one, that's where I want to be."

The light changes, and we cross the street.

"You deserve to be in the spotlight," Daniel says. "You're too beautiful and talented not to be."

Beautiful?

Talented?

I'm in danger of getting a little tipsy on his compliments.

"Don't *you* deserve to be in the spotlight?" I counter, not wanting to let him know that his flattery is totally working on me. "You work hard, and you're good enough to be on the team. Don't you want to be a star?"

"I wouldn't refuse it if it happened. But what I want more than anything is to be part of a team, and I have that. And my scholarship is just as good as our starting quarterback's."

My understanding of athletic scholarships is a little hazy.

"You don't have to be a starter to get a free ride?"

"Nope. The team gets eighty-five scholarships a year. That means second and third stringers, too."

Tuition at Hart is expensive. A full scholarship is a big deal.

"Your family must be so proud of you. Not to mention happy about all the money you're saving them."

"Yeah, I definitely get a lot of family cred for that. My dad died when I was a kid, and my mom raised my sister and me on her own. The football scholarship means my sister can go to college without taking on too much debt."

"You were raised by a single mom?"

He stops walking and looks down at me. The sun is setting in front of us, and a shaft of light makes us both blink.

"You sound surprised," he says.

"I guess I am. I mean . . . I guess I would have expected a guy raised by a single mother to be more . . . to be less . . ."

I remember our ground rule and stop myself. Whatever I ended up saying would have included something about feminism, and that counts as politics.

"You know what? It doesn't matter. Should we keep going?"

"Nope." He gestures behind me. "We're here."

I turn and look.

It's a vegan café that's popular with Hart students. I've never actually eaten here, since I'm a pretty serious carnivore, but I'm willing to give it a go.

"I've always wanted to try this place," I say, and Daniel looks surprised.

"You've never been here before?"

"No. Why?"

"I just thought—" He pauses. "Aren't you from San Francisco?"

I nod.

"I guess I thought someone from San Francisco would be into, uh . . ."

"Healthy food?"

"Yeah."

I grin at him. "Nope. Not at all. But I like trying new things and I'm happy to give this place a shot. A lot of my friends love it."

Daniel's still looking down at me, but now his expression changes. It gets sort of . . . soft.

"What?" I ask, a little nervously. There's something intense about a really big, really tall football player type looking at you like that.

We're facing each other, and now he reaches out to touch the daisy I tucked behind my ear. His fingertips brush the side of my neck, and I shiver.

"It's just the way the sun's hitting you right now. It makes you look like an angel."

The feeling in my chest from the other day comes back. A kind of melting sensation right behind my breastbone.

I don't know what to say. I feel heat coming into my cheeks, and I know I'm blushing.

"Should we go in?"

"Sure."

He opens the door, follows me inside, and asks the waitress who comes to greet us if we can have the little table by the window.

He's really pretty competent at this whole date thing, I'm thinking to myself.

Then I look at the menu.

I struggle to eat vegetables at the best of times, and this is all vegetables. Roasted cauliflower and Brussels sprouts, squash soup, black bean stew, vegan tempeh Reubens, and every kind of salad imaginable.

I hate salad.

But Daniel brought me daisies, he said I looked like an angel, and he picked this place because he thought I'd like it. I'm going to enjoy this meal if it's the last thing I do.

"This all looks great," I lie.

"Yeah," Daniel agrees. He pauses. "What's tempeh?"

"No idea."

"Huh. Okay." He sets his menu down on the table. "So what are you getting?"

I look down and name the first thing I see.

"Spicy tofu lettuce wraps."

I do like spicy food. Maybe the spiciness will help me get down the tofu.

"I think I'll try the tempeh Reuben, even though we don't know what tempeh is. I love Reubens."

We order. And then, after the waitress leaves, we sit and look at each other.

Daniel is so different from the guys I've always gone for. Even with the sexy tousled hair and the sexy short beard, he exudes . . . I don't know. Uprightness, or something. And yet . . .

His shoulders are so broad and so packed with muscle they're straining a little against his shirt. There's a power to Daniel mixed in with his clean-cut vibe. Physical power, of course, but more than that.

Whatever it is, it's not a quality I'm used to seeing in a guy.

At least a minute has passed with neither of us saying anything. The silence is starting to feel awkward. But the more seconds that tick by, the more I feel like I don't know what to say.

We didn't have any trouble talking after drama class. Or, well, arguing. But we didn't have any trouble talking on the walk from Bracton, either, and that wasn't arguing.

But now, for some reason, my mind is blank.

The lighting is a little too bright for date ambience. The wooden chairs aren't very comfortable. And they don't serve alcohol, which has lubricated so many first dates throughout the centuries.

Not that I'd be able to order it even if they did serve alcohol. I'd feel pretty weird pulling out my fake ID in front of a guy who doesn't drink.

A wave of depression goes through me. Daniel and I really don't have anything in common, do we?

Then he leans forward. "Can I ask you a personal question?"

"Sure."

"Why did you decide to come out with me tonight?"

God, why did I?

Of course I know the answer. *Because I'm into you.*

But there's no way I'm going to admit that.

"For the free food," I say, going with flip over truthful.

He smiles. "I'll take that for now. But maybe by the end of the night you'll tell me the real reason."

Doubtful.

The waitress approaches with our dinner, which provides a welcome diversion. Or at least, I think the diversion is welcome until I actually taste it.

It's spicy. But it turns out that the spiciness doesn't help with the tofu, which tastes a little like chewing on the inside of your own cheek.

I chew gamely, but with my stomach already a little tense it's a losing battle. I don't even want to swallow the mess in my mouth.

I do the discreet spit-into-your-napkin thing, hoping Daniel doesn't notice. But when I glance over at him it's obvious he's got troubles of his own.

He's taken a bite of his tempeh Reuben, and the expression on his face is everything I'm feeling and hoping I'm not showing.

When he sees me looking at him he chews and swallows.

"This is pretty good," he says.

A lie. Not a very good lie, either.

And just like that, my depression is gone—replaced by a sudden wave of affection.

It's weird, though. Because the affection is for both of us.

Be Yourself Tonight.

I point at my plate and then at his.

"This is bullshit."

He blinks. "What?"

"It's not food. It's an abomination. Don't you dare take another bite of that thing."

"I—"

"Hang on a sec."

I pull my wallet from my little beaded purse, fish out a twenty, and lay it on the table.

"We're doing a reset, Daniel. Jimmy's Pub is a block away. You're going to buy me a hamburger, and you're going to buy yourself a real Reuben to wash the taste of tempeh out of your mouth forever."

I don't wait for him to respond. I just get up, go around to his side of the table, and hold out my hand.

He looks down at his plate for a second and then back at me. A beat goes by.

Then he takes my hand and I pull him to his feet.

He really does tower over me—even when I'm wearing four inch heels. But as Daniel and I leave the vegan café and step out into the cool night air, the difference doesn't seem like such a big deal.

CHAPTER THIRTEEN

Daniel

I should feel like a failure. I screwed up the first step of planning a date: picking a restaurant the girl will like.

But I don't feel like a failure. As Tamsin and I head for Jimmy's Pub, I feel like a million bucks.

Of course that might just be because we're holding hands.

Tamsin is small and slim, and she's wearing these crazy high heels with all the stability of two chopsticks. They make her seem delicate, fragile, and feminine.

I want to take care of her. I want to make sure she doesn't fall down walking in those shoes. I want to carry her over puddles. I want to stand between her and an invading horde of Visigoths.

And the fact that she just took care of me doesn't change that. It makes this date seem like something we're creating together, like our scenes in drama class.

Maybe improvisation doesn't have to be scary. Maybe it can be exciting.

Thrilling, even.

Jimmy's is Saturday-night crowded, but Tamsin knows one of the waiters and he waves us to a corner booth with a RESERVED sign on it.

"Won't the people who are supposed to get this table be mad?" she asks as we slide onto the vinyl seats.

"Nah," the waiter says. "I keep this one open just in case. Tonight you guys are the just in case. Do you know what you want, or do you need menus?"

"I know what I want," Tamsin says, giving me a look that makes my whole body stand at attention. "What about you, Daniel?"

"I'll take a Reuben," I say to the waiter, my voice sounding kind of rough.

He looks at Tamsin.

"Bacon cheeseburger for me," she tells him.

"Fries on the side?"

"On an epic scale. Bring a giant basket and put it down between us."

"Sure thing."

"You like fries, huh?" I ask as the waiter leaves.

"Indeed I do."

She's smiling at me, and I smile back.

I know what I want, she said.

I probably just imagined there was a double entendre there, but it doesn't matter. Being around Tamsin means I'm going to have sex on the brain, so I'll have to learn to function in a constant state of . . . excitement? Arousal? Hunger? Need?

Yeah. All of that.

The atmosphere in Jimmy's is a lot more date-like than the vegan café. Our corner booth makes it feel like we've got some privacy, even though there are a ton of people in here.

There's music playing and people talking but it's not too loud. It all kind of blends together into background noise, making our space seem even more private, somehow.

The lighting helps, too. It's always pretty dark in Jimmy's, and there's one of those imitation candle things on the table between us. The light it gives out is warm and soft, and it makes Tamsin look like a thirties movie star.

"I like your eye makeup," I hear myself say. "It's perfect for a Saturday night."

Okay, that's a pretty lame compliment. But Tamsin doesn't seem to mind.

"Thanks," she says. She leans forward. "That reminds me. Can I ask you something?"

"Sure."

"It's about Twitter, but it's not political. It's just your handle—@heartofsaturdaynight?"

"What about it?"

"It's the title of a Tom Waits song, and I wondered where you heard that phrase."

I'm not sure what she means. "I heard it from Tom Waits. I mean, it's from that song."

She stares at me. "Your Twitter handle is from a Tom Waits song?"

"Yeah."

"You like Tom Waits?"

"Yeah."

She's still staring at me. After a moment I say,

"Okay, I'm confused. Do you hate Tom Waits?"

She shakes her head slowly. "No. I love him."

I'm still confused. "And that's a bad thing?"

"No, not at all. Just, um, surprising?"

"It is? Why?"

"I guess I wasn't expecting us to have anything in common."

Ah.

"Did you think I only listened to Christian rock or something?"

She starts to smile. "Maybe?"

"Christian rock is terrible."

"Well, *I* know that. But you're the Christian, not me."

"Music *by* Christians isn't terrible, though. Have you ever listened to Chance the Rapper? Or the Mountain Goats?"

She's staring at me again, her eyes big.

"I love Chance the Rapper. I love the Mountain Goats."

I start to say something and then stop.

"What?"

"One of the ground rules tonight was no talk about religion."

She shakes her head. "We're not talking about religion. We're talking about music. And name dropping the Mountain Goats is the seduction equivalent of handing me a brandy on a snowy night and saying 'Baby, it's cold outside.'"

I start to laugh. "Yeah? I had no idea. I'll keep that in mind for next time."

I hear the words as they come out of my mouth, and realize the implication in the same second.

Tamsin does, too. She raises her eyebrows, and a smile plays at the corners of her blood-red lips.

"There's going to be a next time? But I thought this was a once-only deal. Some kind of social experiment. A demonstration of how a real man squires a lady around town."

"Well, I already screwed that up, didn't I? You had to squire me here, after all. We need at least one more date so I can redeem myself."

"No redemption necessary." She rests her forearms on the table, clasps her hands together, and leans toward me. "Say Tom Waits."

I rest my forearms on the table, clasp my hands together, and lean toward her.

"Tom Waits."

A slow smile spreads across her face.

"I am so attracted to you right now."

I know she's joking. Or at least, mostly joking. But at this moment, I'm so attracted to her that every cell in my body feels hard. Like everything in me is in sympathy with the erection that Tamsin, thank God, can't see.

I've been attracted to girls before. But there's a difference between what I felt then and what I'm feeling now.

The other times, it was like the hormones came first. I was a guy with needs, and I had to find a girl I liked enough to justify fooling around.

I know what happened to me when I was twelve had something to do with that. I wanted to replace bad memories with good ones. I wanted to feel like a normal teenager. There was a space in my life for something, and I needed a girl to fill it. Any girl.

This is the opposite. What's surging inside me right now isn't just testosterone. It's a Tamsin-specific hormone bomb.

The lust is so thick and hot and overwhelming I can't think of a damn thing to say. All I can do is sit here, staring at her. Then, thank God, the waiter comes over with our fries.

Maybe it's sublimation, but I'm suddenly starving.

"This is the biggest basket of fries I've ever seen," I say, stuffing three into my mouth at once.

"I know," Tamsin says around her own mouthful. "And they're the best in town, too."

She's right. They're perfectly hot, perfectly crispy, perfectly seasoned.

I can't get enough.

"Tell me about your mom and your sister," Tamsin says after a moment. "That's a normal date thing, right? Asking about family?"

I finish my bite before I answer.

"Sure, that's dating 101. My mom and sister are both great."

"What are their names? And where are you from, by the way?"

The pace of our fry consumption has slowed a little. Tamsin is leaning forward, looking like she's really interested in hearing my answers.

"I'm from Missouri. My mom's name is Donna. My sister is Michelle."

"How old is she? Your sister."

"Sixteen." I pause. "What about your family? Do you have siblings?"

She shakes her head. "No, it's just me and the parents from hell."

"You don't get along with them?"

"No."

This surprises me. I'd pictured a hippie utopia San Francisco childhood for Tamsin, with super-liberal parents she calls by their first names.

"Why not?"

"Because they're terrible." She puts a fry in her mouth, chews, and swallows. "You'd hate them."

"I would? How come?"

"They're like a caricature of coastal elites. Limousine liberals or whatever. They donate to all these causes, but only because they want everyone to think they're generous. They don't really care about anyone but themselves. They're totally selfish. They sent me away to boarding school when I was ten. I cried for weeks and begged them to let me come home, but they wouldn't. The truth is, they don't really like being parents. They don't really like *me*. I mean, I'm sure they think they do. But out of all the shows I was in during high school, do you know how many they came to?"

"I'm kind of afraid the answer is zero."

"That is correct. Zero."

I feel horrible, but Tamsin doesn't seem upset or bitter about any of this. Of course, she's had her whole life to get used to parents who don't want to spend time with her.

Which I just don't understand.

"Your parents are idiots. Plus they're really missing out. You're amazing company, Tamsin."

She stops with a French fry halfway to her mouth and just looks at me. Her eyes are like stars.

"Thanks," she says after a moment.

The waiter comes back then, setting Tamsin's burger in front of her and my Reuben in front of me.

God, it's perfect. Corned beef sliced so thin you can almost see through it, stacked two inches high. Swiss cheese perfectly melted. Tangy sauerkraut and Russian dressing and rye bread toasted golden brown.

I don't look up until I've finished half my sandwich. When I do, Tamsin is eating her burger with an expression of absolute bliss on her face.

"Good, huh?"

She smiles at me. "Better than good."

We finish eating in silence, but it's not awkward. When we're done we sit back with almost identical sighs of contentment, which makes Tamsin giggle.

"Can I ask you something about your parents?"

"Sure."

"How did you cope? I mean, adolescence sucks at the best of times. How did you deal without having a family you could count on?"

Tamsin doesn't answer right away. She pushes her dinner plate to the side—there's nothing on it now but a few sesame seeds from her bun—and takes a French fry from the basket.

Then she says, "I don't know if you really want to hear the answer to that question."

I push my plate to the side, too.

"Why wouldn't I?"

"Because we're on a date. And it's been my experience that the answer to that question tends to be a mood-killer."

I look at her for a moment. She's looking at me, too, and her expression is serious enough that I know she means what she's saying. But what could be bad enough to kill the mood between the two of us right now?

Sex? Drugs? Grand theft auto? What?

"It's not a real date," I remind her. "The stakes couldn't be lower. Tell me."

She studies me a moment longer, and then she shrugs.

"I coped with feeling abandoned by sleeping with guys. A lot of guys."

"Tamsin. I lived in Oscar's dorm freshman year, remember? I know you're not a virgin. And anyway, how would talking about sex be a mood killer on a date?"

Tamsin nibbles on her French fry.

"There's not being a virgin, and then there's being Tamsin Shay, Queen of the Sluts."

I stare at her.

"Jesus. Who called you that?"

Whoever it was, I want to kill them.

"Basically everyone I went to high school with." She puts the fry down, and I get the feeling she's bracing herself for something. "Daniel. You're a sweet guy. But tell me the truth. What would you call a girl who slept with twenty-three guys by the time she was nineteen?"

Twenty-three guys.

Okay, that's a lot. But if Tamsin's waiting for me to recoil in horror or something, she's going to wait a long time.

"I wouldn't call her anything. Because I'm not an asshole."

Her eyes are shining again, and this time I see tears. She blinks them away and smiles a little.

I feel shaken by her reaction. "I can't be the first guy to tell you it doesn't matter."

She shakes her head. "You'd be surprised. But don't you want to know why I've slept with so many guys? Twenty-two of them were in high school, by the way."

"It's none of my business, unless you want to tell me. But you kind of already did. It was because you felt abandoned by your parents." I pause. "But there doesn't have to be a reason. I mean . . . shit. Do you know what I mean?"

She nods, and her eyes are still bright.

"I do. And I appreciate you saying that. But the truth is, if I had a kid sister or a daughter or something, I wouldn't want her to sleep with that many guys in high school. I'd want her to date people she really cares about and who care about her. And chances are, if you sleep with twenty-two people in high school, love isn't taking center stage."

"Are you saying you have regrets?"

She shakes her head. "It's more complicated than that. If I went back in time, I wouldn't make the same decisions. But even though I feel differently about some things now, I was being true to myself back then. I was reckless and rebellious and really, really teenager-y, but I did what I wanted to do. The fact that I want different things now doesn't change that. And what I want now is shaped by what I wanted then, you know? We're all shaped by our past." She pauses. "Rikki said something once. She said if you like who you are now, you can't hate anything that got you there—including your past."

"You're talking about self-acceptance," I hear myself say. "Accepting your own decisions. But what if . . ."

I hesitate. "What if something happened that wasn't your decision. What if someone hurt you when you were too young to decide things for yourself."

I feel my face turning red. What the hell am I doing? But I can tell Tamsin thinks I'm talking about her.

"I've never been hurt like that. Guys pressured me sometimes, sure. But no one ever made me do anything I didn't want to do."

I'm glad to hear it. And I'm even more glad Tamsin doesn't know it's myself I'm talking about.

Because, here's the thing. A girl might feel sorry for a guy who was molested as a kid. She might be furious at the person who did it, sad that it happened, and full of empathy or whatever.

But she won't be attracted to that guy. Because that guy is a victim, and no matter how enlightened someone thinks they are, guys aren't supposed to be victims. Especially of sexual assault.

The whole point of me taking Tamsin out tonight was to show her what an old-fashioned date looks like. With an old-fashioned guy.

Old-fashioned guys are strong and confident and whole. They can take care of other people. Protect them.

They never need to be protected themselves.

But I don't have to think about that now. Tamsin doesn't know about my past, and she never will. We're on a date, whether it's real or fake or some combination of both, and I'm happier than I've been in a long time.

I rest my forearms on the table, clasp my hands together, and lean toward her.

"Say Tom Waits."

Tamsin rests her forearms on the table, clasps her hands together, and leans toward me.

"Tom Waits."

I lower my voice. "I am so attracted to you right now."

Her lipstick must be smudge-proof, because even after her burger and fries it's perfect.

Her mouth curves up in a smile. "I know."

The waiter comes over with our check. I pull out my wallet, lay down two twenties, and slide out of the booth.

I hold out my hand to help Tamsin up. As she gets to her feet I ask,

"How can you walk on those heels?"

"It's a combination of skill and desire. Basically, it's a mystery." She pauses. "Are we going home now?"

She sounds disappointed, which thrills me.

"My original date plan included a stop at the ice cream place near campus."

"Ooh, perfect."

It would have been perfect. But when we get outside, it's drizzling.

The ice cream place has a window for service and outdoor tables. That's not going to work.

Damn.

"How about a rain check on the ice cream?" I ask.

We're protected at the moment, standing under the big awning in front of Jimmy's.

Tamsin squeezes my hand. "We never did resolve the question of a second date. Does this mean there's going to be one?"

I want there to be. God, I want there to be.

But then I hear a voice inside my head.

You and Tamsin don't belong together. Enjoy this one perfect night and leave it at that.

Screw the voice inside my head.

"Yeah," I say, throwing caution to the wind. "There's going to be a second date."

I unbutton my long-sleeved shirt, pull it off, and drape it over Tamsin's shoulders. I'm wearing a T-shirt underneath, so I'm fine. But Tamsin needs protection from the rain.

"It's only drizzling," she says, but she slips her arms into the sleeves.

They're way too long for her, and she looks adorable.

"Ready to brave the elements?" I ask.

"Ready, Captain."

Then we step out from under the awning and head back toward campus.

CHAPTER FOURTEEN

Tamsin

Daniel's shirt is warm, making me feel like I'm walking in a cocoon of kindness and chivalry.

And it's sexy as hell in here.

I'm so sure Daniel will break his no-kissing, no-fooling-around rule that I surreptitiously send Rikki the one-word text we agreed on in case I wanted the room to myself tonight.

Jackpot.

She sends me a thumbs-up emoji, meaning she'll spend the night with Sam.

Daniel and I hold hands all the way back to Bracton, and the body heat he gives off bodes well for the night to come.

He's hot-blooded, is what I'm saying. Insert suggestive eyebrow-wiggling here.

The drizzle turns into a steady shower by the time we get back to the dorm, and our water-logged state makes my invitation even easier.

"You're coming in, right?" I say, after we climb the stairs and stop outside my door. "You can dry off and hang out while you wait for the rain to stop."

I've never been more confident of getting a *Hell, yes* in response to a proposition. Daniel and I are facing each other, and with his hair wet and his T-shirt damp and a drop of rain sliding down his cheek, all I can think about is getting him inside and out of his clothes.

"That's okay," he says. "I don't mind the rain."

I blink, almost convinced I heard him wrong.

"What?"

He reaches out and plucks the daisy from my hair.

"I'm going to take this with me," he says. "Not that I'll need any help thinking about you on my way home."

That's pretty romantic. But at the same time, the bottom line is that he's not coming in.

I don't know what to say. I've never felt so rejected and not-rejected at the exact same time.

"We've got an away game next week," he continues. "So how is two weeks from tonight for our next date?"

He can wait two weeks to see me again? And he's not even going to kiss me goodnight?

The scales are tipping from not-rejected to rejected.

"Okay," I say. My voice sounds small, and I hate that. I hate how I'm feeling right now.

"Goodnight, Tamsin. I had an amazing time, and I can't wait to do it again."

"Goodnight, Daniel."

And that's that.

I stand there staring after him as he walks down the hall and disappears into the stairwell. Then I go into my room and over to the window. It overlooks the main entrance of the building, and I wait for Daniel to come out the front door.

It was a perfect night. The best date I've ever had.

Well, the only date I've ever had. I went to boarding school, where dating consists of finding places on school grounds to have sex. And Oscar, as Daniel himself pointed out, was never the romantic date night type.

Daniel had a good time too. I'm sure he did. I didn't just imagine those moments of connection—or those moments of lust. But how could he walk away without so much as a kiss?

I lean against the window glass. "O, wilt thou leave me so unsatisfied?" I murmur.

That's Romeo's line, of course, from the famous balcony scene.

What satisfaction canst thou have tonight? Juliet responds.

Th' exchange of thy love's faithful vow for mine, Romeo tells her.

I don't want that, obviously. Daniel and I are just getting to know each other, and while we have more in common than I would have guessed twenty-four hours ago, there are still way more differences than similarities between us.

It's ridiculous to think Daniel and I would ever declare our love to each other, much less do it tonight.

But I am unsatisfied. *Extremely* unsatisfied.

The door below me opens, and Daniel comes out. He's in his white T-shirt, and I remember that I'm still wearing his red button-down shirt.

The rain is coming down even harder now, and I expect him to hurry away toward home.

Instead, he stops in the middle of the sidewalk and just stands there, his face lifted to the sky. He's getting soaked. One of his hands is in his pocket and the other is holding something to his heart.

The daisy. *My* daisy.

My heart starts to pound.

I turn away from the window. And then, as fast as I can on four-inch heels, I rush out of my room and down the stairs.

I'm terrified Daniel will be gone by the time I go out the front door. But he's still standing there in the pouring rain, and I call out his name.

"Daniel!"

He turns.

I was going to start by giving him back his shirt. That's all. But the moment I see his face, wet and surprised and adorable, that plan goes out the window.

I come at him full-speed, but I don't knock him over. I barrel into him and throw my arms around his neck, and then I'm kissing him.

His arms wrap me up and I'm surrounded. He's wet with rainwater and warm with the blood pumping through his veins and every inch of his body is hard, hard, hard.

His kiss is a hundred different things. Rough and soft, warm and cool, hungry and tender and fierce all at once.

I'm overwhelmed. My breasts are crushed against his chest and my heart is beating like thunder and my knees wouldn't hold me up if I wasn't clinging to Daniel's shoulders.

The stroke of his tongue inside my mouth is electric. He tastes like rain and something else, something dark and rich and wild.

He can't kiss me any deeper. He can't kiss me any harder.

And then, somehow, he does.

I'm drowning in rain, drowning in Daniel, drowning in the desire that floods through me in waves.

I don't want to stop. Ever. The fever is so hot I expect the raindrops landing on us to sizzle and steam. It feels like we could dissolve into clouds and water and—

"Tamsin."

Daniel breaks the kiss and says my name. His voice is rough and ragged, and when I open my eyes and look up at him, he doesn't look anything like the clean-cut boy I've been ogling the past week.

Standing there in a rain-soaked tee, his body seems bigger and broader than when he's wearing a button-down shirt. His pupils are so dilated his eyes look black, and they're so intense they seem to burn into me.

His hands are on my shoulders now. It feels like he could snap my bones in two, like he could squeeze just a little and crush me to powder.

All that power. All that strength. And he's fighting something—I can see it in his eyes and in his jaw. I can feel it in his hands, shaking even as he grips my shoulders.

The rain has let up a little. It's softer now, a gentle fall of droplets from the sky. Daniel leans forward, slowly, and kisses the wetness from my forehead, my cheeks, my lips.

The brush of his mouth on my skin makes me tremble. My eyes flutter closed and he kisses my eyelids, too.

Then his hands are in my hair. It's heavy and wet with the rain, and his fingers sliding into it makes my scalp tingle.

He tilts my head back, and now his mouth is on my neck.

Oh, God.

Someone is moaning, and I'm pretty sure it's me.

I slide my hands down from Daniel's shoulders to fist in his T-shirt. I arch my head back as he drags his lips down my throat.

My heart is thundering in my chest, my pulse beating like a drum. My body doesn't feel like flesh and bone anymore. I'm all need and hunger and quivering desire, electric longing and sizzling heat.

Daniel pulls back for a moment and I open my eyes. For an instant we stare at each other.

Then I grab his wet T-shirt by the hem and pull it up and off.

"Tamsin," he rasps out, staring down at me.

He's naked from the waist up, and sweet mother of God.

I drop the T-shirt to the ground and reach for him. His bare skin is warm and smooth and damp, and as I shape my palms to the heavy bands of muscle on his shoulders, his arms, his chest, I wonder how his hands in my hair and his mouth on my throat could have been so gentle. How do you leash this much strength? How do you restrain this much power?

I don't know where his restraint comes from. All I know is that right now, I don't have any.

I step in close and slide my arms around his waist. Then I press my lips to his chest, tasting skin and raindrops and the heat of his blood, pumping just below the surface.

His hands are in my hair again, his grip a little harder this time. My hands slide down to his hips as I press my lower body to his, and—

He.

Is.

So.

Hard.

He starts to shift back a little, but I'm not having that. I slip my hands into his back pockets and pull him in close again, and the entire length of his hard-on is cradled against my stomach.

My stomach takes note by swooping and tightening and trembling like butterfly wings.

My whole body is doing that, basically. Shaking and quivering and—

"Geez, you guys. Get a room."

Daniel and I both freeze. The voice came from behind him, and I rise up on my tiptoes to look over his shoulder. Two freshmen girls are standing a few yards away. They're staring at us from under the shelter of a big umbrella, and as soon as they catch my eye, they giggle and hurry away.

"Fucking freshmen," I mutter.

But they did make one very important point.

I pull back and look up at Daniel.

"I actually have a room," I say. "Rikki's with her boyfriend." I take a breath. "Stay with me tonight."

It's a straight-up proposition. I'm not pretending to be coy or subtle or anything but what I am: a woman who wants a man.

A woman who wants *this* man.

But I don't realize how much I'm putting on the line until Daniel says,

"I can't."

I stare at him. It's one thing to ask a guy in, sort of casually, and have him say no. It's another to share a kiss like that one, invite a guy to spend the night with you, and have him say no.

I should play it cool. But that kiss scraped me raw, and I can't play anything but myself.

"I don't understand. Are you saying you don't want me?"

There's an echo in those words of the girl I swore I'd never be again. The girl who used to ask, plaintively, why a guy was ending things. *Why are you breaking up with me? Don't you want me any more?*

Daniel looks down at me for a long moment. Then he takes a deep breath.

"I've never wanted anything like I want you right now."

His voice is rough. His eyes are glittering like a wolf's in the dark.

It's obvious he's speaking no more than the simple truth.

His words should make me feel better, but they don't.

Because now I'm confused. And frustrated.

"So stay with me. Stay the night."

He drags his hands through his wet hair. The action makes his biceps and triceps bunch up, and I feel a twinge of lust deep in my belly.

"I can't."

"Why?"

He just shakes his head. I see my own frustration reflected in his face, and now I'm even more confused.

"Is it a religious thing?" I ask, casting around for some reason that makes sense. "Is it—"

Suddenly another possibility occurs to me.

I take a deep breath. "Daniel. Are you a virgin?"

As soon as I ask that question I wish I hadn't. He sort of rears back and then freezes, staring down at me.

"What if I am?" he asks after a moment. "Would you see that as some sort of character flaw?"

His voice is tight, and I wish more than anything I could take back the question.

"No. Of course not. I just—"

"You just need a reason for a guy not wanting to sleep with you on the first date?"

There are a lot of things that could be behind that question, and I don't like any of them.

"Are you saying there's something wrong with me for *wanting* to sleep with you? Are you calling me easy, Mr. I-Never-Slut-Shame-Women?"

Up until this moment, my lust for Daniel was like a hot water bottle. I was feeling warm—deliciously warm. But now, for the first time, my body notices that the air is cold and I'm soaking wet.

I shiver.

Daniel sees. "You should go inside," he says gruffly. "You'll catch cold if you stay out here."

He bends down and grabs his wadded up T-shirt from the ground.

"Daniel—"

He straightens up again and looks at me. "I'll see you in class on Tuesday."

We can't leave things like this. We just can't. I'm angry and frustrated and sad and confused. How could such an amazing night turn so sour so fast?

"Daniel—"

He shakes his head. "Let's not. Okay? I'll see you later, Tamsin. Thanks for coming out with me tonight."

And then he turns and walks away.

CHAPTER FIFTEEN

Daniel

Well, that was awful.

And wonderful.

The best date I've ever been on.

And the worst.

Tamsin.

Tamsin.

Tamsin.

Her name is like a refrain I can't let go of, a song playing on an endless loop.

Tamsin.

She invited me up to her room, and I said no.

Fuck.

If I needed any more proof that I'm too screwed up to have a relationship, I just got it.

I can't think of anything I want less than to put on my soaking wet T-shirt, but I don't want to walk around bare-chested either. So I pull it on, and it's every bit as cold and clammy as I figured it would be.

How can a night go from transcendent to tragic in a single minute?

Well, maybe not tragic. But definitely off the rails.

It's all my fault. I knew I was playing with fire the moment I asked Tamsin out.

She's like an open flame. And when I'm around her, I feel like a rag soaked in gasoline.

You should have spent the night with her.

I tell the voice inside my head to shut up. How the hell could I spend the night with Tamsin? She already asked me if I'm a virgin. There's no way she wouldn't know the truth if I tried to sleep with her.

A girl like Tamsin deserves a guy who knows what he's doing. A guy she doesn't need to educate like some kind of sexual charity case. A guy who won't freeze up if she touches his cock.

She deserves someone experienced. Someone confident. Someone who can take the lead.

Because when it comes to relationships, a man should take the lead. I know that's old-fashioned, but it's what I believe.

I grew up with a single mom and a sister. I've seen women in action in church and community groups. I see the way they put other people first, the way take care of everyone except themselves.

I saw Tamsin do that with Oscar, the least deserving guy on the planet. All the little things she did for him that he took for granted.

When it comes to romance, I think the guy should do things for the girl. Open doors. Bring her flowers. Pay the check.

And rock her world in bed.

The rain stops just as I reach my house. When I open the front door, I see Trace and Beeker on the couch playing Assassin's Creed.

The three of us really know how to have a wild Saturday night.

If I could I'd sneak up to my room, but the stairs are on the other side of the living room. I cross in front of Trace and Beeker without saying anything, hoping they're too focused on the game to pay attention to me.

No such luck.

"Danny boy!"

That's Trace's nickname for me when he's not using Galahad.

"Hey," I say, pausing at the bottom of the stairs.

Beeker is staring at me. "What the hell happened to you? You look like you took a shower with your clothes on. Didn't you have a date tonight?"

"I did. It's over. I walked home in the rain. See you guys tomorrow, okay?"

I make it maybe three steps.

"Oh, hell no," Beeker says. "Tell us about the date. The date with—what was her name?"

"Tamsin."

"Yeah. Tamsin."

They've paused the game, and now Trace leans forward and grabs a bottle of something—bourbon, maybe—from the coffee table, pouring a shot into a plastic cup.

"Want one?" he asks me, like he always does.

I always say no, and Trace always leaves it at that. He's never given me a hard time about not drinking, which is one of the good things about him.

I don't have some kind of moral objection to alcohol. I just don't drink it myself—not since my neighbor offered me a beer when I was twelve years old and I took it, feeling ten feet tall and badass as I chugged it down.

I haven't taken a drink since. But now I hear myself say,

"Yeah. I'll have one."

Beeker and Trace both stare at me. Then Trace grabs an empty cup and fills it half full of amber liquid.

"Here you go. Man, you must have had a hell of a night. Was it really good or really bad?"

"Both," I say, coming over and taking the cup from Trace. "But I don't want to talk about that. Are the West Coast games over? How did Oregon and UCLA do?"

There are two things I have no intention of doing. One, getting drunk. Two, talking about Tamsin.

So, of course, I get drunk and talk about Tamsin.

Trace and Beeker are pretty decent, all things considered. They don't laugh at me too much, and they make sure I get upstairs and into bed before I crash.

They're not so bad, those guys. Even Trace.

The first thing I do when I wake up—after I brush my teeth, since my mouth tastes like a dumpster—is check my Twitter DMs. I forgot to get Tamsin's phone number last night, which means Twitter is the only way we can get hold of each other.

I open the app and check the little envelope.

Nothing.

I lay down in bed again and stare at the ceiling. I don't remember much of my drunken conversation with Trace and Beeker, but I remember every detail of my time with Tamsin.

I fucked everything up at the end, and I can't think of a way to fix it.

I could apologize, of course. That part would be easy enough. But what I can't fix is the reason I acted the way I did.

I can't fix being screwed up about sex. I can't fix being a virgin *with* Tamsin unless I sleep with someone who *isn't* Tamsin, and even if I wasn't screwed up about sex, there's no way I could sleep with a girl I don't care about just to be comfortable sleeping with the girl I actually do care about.

What happened at the end of our date was a symptom of things I can't change. So what good would it do to apologize?

Maybe it's better that I don't have Tamsin's phone number. Maybe it's better that she's not DMing me. Maybe it's better that we go back to being scene partners and frenemies or whatever we were before last night.

And maybe I'm a big fucking liar.

Yeah, I probably am. But going back to the way things were is all I've got.

* * *

It's Tuesday night and I'm keyed up. I thought I might run into Tamsin before drama class, but I didn't. So this will be the first time we've seen each other since Saturday night.

On the way to the theater, I decide I'll let Tamsin set the tone. If she ignores me, fine. If she wants to talk, great. I was the one who asked her out, and I'm the one responsible for how it ended. I'll let Tamsin decide what happens next.

When I get to class, Tamsin's already there. She's sitting between Izzy and Charlie in the third row.

What's it going to be? Will she ignore me, or will she talk to me?

It's sort of in-between. She doesn't say anything, but she nods. The way you acknowledge an acquaintance.

I nod back. And even though I told myself I'd accept whatever attitude Tamsin took, that one moment of cool eye contact really stings.

Our kiss Saturday night shook me to my core. *Tamsin* shook me to my core. So much that I drank alcohol for the first time in eight years and babbled about her to my housemates.

But it looks like Tamsin wasn't affected the same way.

It shouldn't bother me. After all, I decided it would be better if we went back to the way things were. I should be happy, right?

Except I'm not happy. In fact, as Joan comes in and starts talking about dramatic tension and character conflict, I feel my own tension rising.

I want to talk to Tamsin. I want her to say that our kiss was the best one of her life, because it sure as hell was mine.

But who am I kidding? Tamsin slept with twenty-two people before she even got to college, while I've slept with a grand total of none. And yeah, I've fooled around with girls—two in high school and five here at Hart—but the fact is, Tamsin has a lot more experience than I do.

Chances are that kiss *wasn't* the best one of her life.

And now, for the first time, I get why a guy might resent his girlfriend's sexual past.

It's not about her. It's about his insecurity. But the fact that it's a stupid, fucked up way to feel doesn't make it less real.

Or less depressing.

I'm so depressed, in fact, that I don't even feel nervous when Joan calls me up on stage.

I feel reckless.

I wasn't really listening to her lecture about tension and conflict, but it's too late to do anything about that. I'll just focus on whatever setup she gives me.

"All right," she says. "The title of today's scene is, Confess Your Unpopular Opinion. It can be anything at all. What's your unpopular opinion, Daniel?"

Most of what I believe is probably unpopular in here. But I don't want to pick something random. I want to talk about something that actually matters to me. Something real.

I look out at the audience, and say:

"I believe in God."

Joan's eyebrows go up. She's wearing a red sweatshirt, which makes her look even more like Mrs. Claus than usual.

"Okay, then. Who wants to take the opposite side of the argument?"

Tamsin gets to her feet. "I'll do it."

She comes up on stage, turns to face the audience, and bows dramatically.

"Just call me Tamsin, Godless Atheist."

That gets a laugh, but not from me. I can already tell Tamsin won't be taking this scene seriously.

But that's not something I can control.

Joan hops off the stage and takes her usual seat in the middle of the front row.

"Okay, Daniel. Tell us what you believe."

Wow. Talk about a tall order.

Then again, what the hell do I have to lose?

If there's one thing I learned in high school, it's that you'll always be punished for sincerity. The only way to stay safe from ridicule is to never take anything seriously, never say what you really feel, and always sound cynical.

The day you decide you're not going to do that is the day you grow up.

I turn to face Tamsin. She's wearing an electric blue skirt, black boots, and a Ramones T-shirt so old the white lettering is flaking off.

She looks gorgeous.

I take a deep breath. "I believe in God's love. I believe in God's forgiveness. I believe that while human beings will let us down, God never will."

Tamsin's gray eyes narrow, and she folds her arms. Her posture seems oddly defensive, as though what I just said is some kind of attack.

"So you believe in a big sky bully, sitting up there and judging us mortals?"

"Wow. No. That's pretty much the opposite of what I believe. Did you miss the part about love and forgiveness?"

"That implies we've done things we need to be forgiven for."

"Well, haven't we? We're all sinners. Or are you saying you're perfect?"

"Oh, I'm far from perfect. But I don't need God's forgiveness—or anyone else's."

Her chin is up, and she looks defiant.

Does she think *I'm* judging her?

"No human being has the right to judge," I say. "Our job is to forgive each other and love each other."

I'm trying to get past Tamsin's defensiveness, and I figure talking in a mild way about being non-judgmental and loving your neighbor is a good way to do that.

"That's definitely the most patronizing thing I've heard this week. But of course it's still early."

So much for my theory.

"Come on, Tamsin. What's patronizing about saying we shouldn't judge each other? And that we're supposed to be loving and forgiving?"

She's looking more pissed off every second, and I don't understand why.

"I don't need your forgiveness. Or God's."

I give the answer I've heard my minister give so many times before.

"Whether or not you need it, you have it."

Her head jerks a little, as though I just slapped her in the face.

"Well, isn't that sweet. No . . . that's not the word I'm looking for. What is it? Oh, right." She takes a breath. "*Sanctimonious.* You can take your forgiveness and shove it up your ass, you sanctimonious prick."

I stare at her. What the hell is going on? I feel like I'm walking blindfolded through a minefield.

"I'm supposed to tell you what I believe. Okay, well, this is what I believe. I believe that God's love can heal anything. I believe His grace is infinite and always available. But whether or not we let it into our lives is up to us."

Tamsin doesn't say anything to that. We just stand there for a moment, staring at each other.

"And . . . end scene," Joan says. "Good job, you two. Nice job drawing out the tension and conflict. Okay, who's next?"

Tamsin's out the door the minute class is over. I'm caught flat-footed, with no chance to catch her—not with students milling around in front of the door, laughing and chatting.

Instead of trying to force my way through the crowd to run after Tamsin, I stay in my seat until everyone's gone.

I feel frustrated. But the truth is, it's probably better if Tamsin and I don't talk right now. It feels like there's a chasm between us—a chasm that Tamsin obviously has no desire to cross.

Finally I leave my seat and head for the door. But before I get there, I stop and look at the stage. Then I climb the three stairs that lead up to it, go to the center where Tamsin and I did our scene, and look out at the empty seats.

"We have traveled so far, and my wife is very tired. Is there any room at your inn?"

"You know, most people launch right into Hamlet when they're alone on a stage."

CHAPTER SIXTEEN

Daniel

I whip my head around, and there's Tamsin. She's leaning against the doorframe with her hands on her hips.

"What is that from?" she asks. "A Charlie Brown Christmas?"

She doesn't look mad, and she did come back to talk to me. That's got to be a good sign, right? Maybe things between us aren't as bleak as I thought.

"Close. It's the nativity scene."

"Seriously? Did you do the Christmas pageant at your church, or something?"

"Yeah. Every year." I pause. "Are you going to make fun of me?"

"I'm not *that* much of a bitch."

That makes me smile.

Tamsin comes over and sits down in the front row. "It seems like a church Christmas pageant would be an awful experience. I mean, no one really wants to be there, do they? And you've got little kids running around and people singing and acting who can't sing or act."

I come forward to sit on the apron of the stage, my legs dangling over the edge like I'm Jack sitting in the giant's chair.

"The first year I did it, I was just trying to help out my minister. The kid who usually played Joseph had moved away and no one else wanted to do it. So I volunteered—with a strong nudge from my mom, who's very community-minded. It was pretty much like you described, plus a really cheesy set and costumes. Take any cliché you can think of about a local church doing a Christmas play, and that was us."

Tamsin kicks off her boots and tucks her feet up under her. "How did the performance go?"

I put my hands on the edge of the stage, my fingers curving around the smooth wood.

"It was Christmas Eve. The pageant is always at five o'clock because of the little kids. You'd think that would make it less magical, right? Compared to the midnight service. I mean, anything happening at midnight has its own built-in magic. But it's dark by five o'clock in December, and it was snowing that day. Not too much—just the perfect amount to be beautiful without making the roads bad.

"I got to the church a little late and I had to hurry to get ready. I put on my Joseph robe and strapped on my Joseph beard, and I noticed that we all looked pretty dumb wearing our costumes over jeans and sneakers. But I told myself it would all be over in a couple hours.

"Then we came up from the church basement to take our places.

"There were no electric lights on—only candles. Candles everywhere. I don't know if you've ever been in a big space lit by candlelight, but it's incredible. The light flickers, and it feels like you're under water.

"And there was this amazing scent in the air. Someone had brought in real frankincense and myrrh for the wise men, and it smelled . . . I don't know. Ancient and mysterious and holy.

"Then the choir director sat down at the piano—our church doesn't have an organ—and started playing carols to warm up before the show.

"I loved Christmas carols even before that night. But hearing them in a church full of candlelight and frankincense was something else. Then the congregation came in and we started the pageant, and I just . . . felt like Joseph. I felt like a poor man with a pregnant wife. We went to place after place, but no one would take us in. We'd traveled so far and she was so tired, and all I wanted to do was take care of her.

"And I did, with God's help. We didn't find a palace or silk sheets or anything like that, but we found a stable warm from the animals in it, and warm with the love of angels and shepherds and wise men from far away. Ordinary human love and the love of God, come together in one moment of time."

There's one detail of the story I don't tell Tamsin. The night of the Christmas pageant was eight months after my neighbor molested me.

I'd been to church at least thirty times since. Eight months of Sundays. And every time we bowed our heads in prayer, I'd ask God why He let it happen. How He could allow such evil in the world.

But the only answer I found was intellectual. The idea of free will. Which basically means, as far as I could tell back then, that God doesn't interfere with what human beings do to each other. Because for free will to be a real thing with real consequences, it has to allow for evil as well as good.

That's when I found out that "free will" is a really unsatisfying answer when you're suffering.

But that Christmas Eve, I wasn't asking God why He lets bad things happen. I wasn't asking any questions at all, really. Something about the candles and the frankincense and the kids all around me in their robes and sneakers, singing Christmas carols at the top of their lungs, just got to me.

I was there, in the moment, feeling something flow through me.

God's love.

I know I'll never be able to convey that moment to Tamsin. Not really. I still don't understand it myself. I just know that after that night, I've never doubted that God is with me, and has always been with me, even on the worst day of my life.

When I finish talking, Tamsin doesn't say anything right away. She just looks at me, and I wonder what she's thinking.

"Is that the play you talked about last week? The one you thought about when you signed up for this class?"

"Yeah."

With her feet tucked under her like that, she looks younger than she is. With my legs dangling over the edge of the stage, I feel younger than I am.

"I wish I'd been there," Tamsin says. "I've never seen a nativity play, but I do love Christmas carols."

"Have you ever been to a Christmas service?"

She shakes her head. "My mom's Jewish, which means I'm Jewish, and my dad isn't anything in particular."

I didn't know Tamsin was Jewish. "Do you go to temple?"

"Not now. We used to go once in a while, whenever my grandmother was in town. I remember this one time she took me to Yom Kippur services. That's the Day of Atonement, and there's this part where everyone confesses their sins. While we're doing that, we actually beat our breasts. There was something really cathartic about that service. All those people, feeling something together. Confessing their sins together, asking forgiveness together, promising to do better together. It made me think about the whole idea of catharsis in Greek drama. The idea that the audience participates in a play through their emotions—their pity and fear—and that the experience can heal you."

I smile a little. "So you don't believe in the power of God's forgiveness, but you do believe in the power of art to heal?"

"Pretty much."

"What made you want to be an actor? Was it a play you went to?"

She nods. "*The Tempest.* I was fourteen, and a Shakespeare group came to our school. It hit me the way your Christmas play hit you. Like magic."

"I probably read *The Tempest* in high school, but I don't remember it." I jump down from the stage. "Can you do a speech from it?"

"Are you kidding? Of course I can. I'm a drama queen, Daniel."

Tamsin puts her boots back on and goes up on stage, while I sit down where she just was.

The seat is still warm from her body.

She comes forward and looks out at an imaginary audience. I half expect her to make a joke of it, hamming it up with dramatic gestures and a booming voice, but when she begins her voice is quiet.

"Our revels now are ended. These our actors,
As I foretold you, were all spirits and
Are melted into air, into thin air.
And like the baseless fabric of this vision,
The cloud-capped towers, the gorgeous palaces,
The solemn temples, the great globe itself—
Yea, all which it inherit—shall dissolve,
And like this insubstantial pageant faded,
Leave not a rack behind. We are such stuff
As dreams are made on, and our little life
Is rounded with a sleep."

Goosebumps prickle my skin.

"Wow," I say after a moment. "That was good, Tamsin."

"Thanks."

She comes forward and sits where I was, her legs dangling off the edge of the stage.

"That's one of my favorite speeches in all of Shakespeare. I'm surprised you like it, though. I mean, it's pretty atheistic, isn't it? It's talking about the transience of life without saying anything about an afterlife or heaven. Just that we're here and then we're gone, with nothingness before and after."

I shake my head. "I don't know about that. It could be saying that mortal life will dissolve, while eternal life might still be there in the background."

"That sounds like wishful thinking. Which, by the way, is my whole objection to organized religion."

She grins at me, and I stick my tongue out at her. Then I say,

"Hey, Tamsin?"

"What?"

"Why were you so angry during our scene? We're talking about all the same stuff now, but you're not yelling at me."

She raises her eyebrows. "That was acting."

I raise my eyebrows, too. "Really?"

"Okay, fine. I might have been a little mad at you, but it wasn't about the scene. It was because of Saturday night."

I wasn't going to bring Saturday night up at all. Not unless she did.

"Since you mention it, do you mind telling me what's so bad about not wanting to sleep with a girl on a first date?"

"If you tell me what's so bad about *wanting* to sleep with someone on a first date."

"There's nothing bad about it. I just didn't want to."

"You mean you didn't want *me*."

"That's not—"

"Why can't you just say it? A kiss like a volcano, and you didn't want anything more? We both know the reason. The truth is, I'm not pure enough to touch your penis. You'll go out with me, but just to show me how a real gentleman does things. You'll even kiss me—although that part was my idea. But you won't sleep with me. Because I'm tainted."

Is that really what she thinks?

If anyone in here is tainted, it's me. I may be sure God can love people no matter what, but I'm not so confident about human beings.

There's nothing sexy about being a victim of molestation. If Tamsin knew the truth, she'd feel sorry for me, because she's a good person.

But she wouldn't want to date me. Because *I'm* tainted.

I can't tell her any of that, and I can't think of anything else to say. But before the silence gets awkward, Tamsin shakes her head.

"I'm sorry. I didn't mean to talk about this. That's not why I came back to look for you."

"Why did you come back?"

She sighs. "To say we should forget about Saturday night. Or at least, we should forget it was supposed to be a date. We should remember that we both love Tom

Waits, that we hate vegan food, and that the French fries at Jimmy's are the best in town. And we should be friends."

Friends.

Well, that's great. That's what I think, too.

Isn't it?

There are so many reasons for us not to be a couple. All the differences between us. All the ways I'm screwed up.

So why don't those things seem real right now?

Sitting here staring at Tamsin, there's only one thing in the world that seems real.

I get up and cross the space between us.

"I don't want to be friends with you."

She looks hurt for just a moment, and then her chin comes up.

"Well, then—"

"I want to be more than friends with you."

Her eyes widen. I step close, my thighs touching her knees, and when her legs part I step into the cradle between them.

She's wearing a skirt, and it's up around her hips now. The only thing separating my hard-on from her body are my pants and her underwear.

Tamsin stares at me, her lips parted. I can actually see her pupils dilate.

Her breath is coming faster. There are only a few inches between her mouth and mine.

"I don't believe you," she whispers. "If that was true, you wouldn't have—"

I lean in and kiss her.

Everything about her is soft. Her lips, her skin, her breasts against my chest.

She's so soft it almost kills me.

The kiss is gentle at first, because I'm half-afraid of breaking her.

But when her legs wrap around my waist and her arms lock around my neck, everything changes.

Our mouths open and our tongues meet. Electricity rocks my whole body.

It feels like we're trying to get inside each other, and for the first time in my life I'm not afraid of that.

When this kiss started I was afraid of bruising her. But now all I can think of is devouring her.

I can't get enough. When she breaks the kiss, gasping for breath, I drag my mouth down her neck to the hollow of her throat.

I get the whole vampire thing now. Because I want to bite Tamsin right here, right where her pulse is thrumming. I want to drink her essence until we're made of the same thing. Until we breathe the same air and bleed the same blood.

I kiss the place instead, tasting the hint of salt on her skin.

She shudders in my arms.

"Daniel . . ."

The sound of her saying my name explodes my few remaining brain cells. Before I know what's happening she's on her back and I'm above her, my body crushing hers, my cock as desperate as the rest of me.

Maybe something's changed. Maybe enough time has gone by. Maybe I'm finally ready to have sex with someone.

No, not someone.

Tamsin.

But then she reaches down between us and takes me in her hand, and I jump back like I was shot.

Fuck.

It happened so fast. My body reacted before I could.

Fuck.

I'm standing a foot or two back from the stage now, staring at Tamsin and panting. She raises herself up on her elbows and stares back at me, her face flushed and her lips swollen. Her hair is mussed and her skirt is up around her waist and she looks so beautiful right now I can't stand it.

"Sorry," I manage to say, and she shakes her head.

"No, you're right. Someone could walk in any second. We just got carried away."

She thinks I was worried about someone catching us. Thank God for that.

She sits up now, straightening her skirt and running her hands through her hair. She takes a deep breath and lets it out slowly, and I'm suddenly very conscious of her small, perfect breasts under her Ramones shirt.

I remember exactly how they felt crushed against my chest.

"Do you . . ." she pauses, her expression uncertain.

"What?"

She looks like she's taking her courage in both hands.

"Do you want to come back to my dorm? Rikki's probably staying with Sam tonight. We could, um, have the place to ourselves."

I'm so concerned with my own hang-ups it would be easy to miss the look on Tamsin's face. But I force myself to focus on her, because I don't want to screw up again.

She's risking rejection. She's totally vulnerable right now.

Don't fuck this up.

I close the distance between us again and take her right hand in both of mine. Then I raise it to my lips and kiss it.

When I meet her eyes again, she's smiling.

"Such a romantic."

I keep hold of her hand. It's small and warm and soft in mine.

"Do you believe I want to be more than friends with you?"

She nods slowly.

"Okay, good. Because here's the thing. I *want* to be more than friends with you. But I can't."

She looks confused, but at least she doesn't look hurt or rejected.

"Why?"

"Because I'm a virgin."

Her eyes widen.

"You . . ." She stops and tries again. "You are?"

I nod.

"Okay," she says after a moment. "I'm trying to wrap my mind around this. Just give me a minute here."

"Take all the time you need. But you asked me if I was a virgin on Saturday night. A part of you must have suspected."

"If a part of me suspected, the other part thought I was crazy. I mean, you're the sexiest guy I've ever met, and it seems insane that no woman has jumped your bones yet. But aside from that, why would being a virgin mean we can't be together?"

I smile slowly. "I'm the sexiest guy you've ever met?"

"Can you answer my question, please?"

I can't tell her all the truth. But I can tell her part of the truth.

"A guy is supposed to know what he's doing."

She stares at me. "Seriously?"

"Yeah."

She thinks about that for a moment.

"Okay. Well. Granting that premise—which I don't, by the way—I have a convenient solution to this problem. Once we have sex, you'll know what you're doing."

God, I wish it was that simple.

"I see where you're coming from. But, Tamsin . . . think about it for a second. You've got experience and I don't. If we sleep together, you'll be like my teacher or something. That's not sexy or romantic or—"

She was smiling at me a moment ago, but now her smile fades.

"So I'm being punished for having sexual experience."

"No! That's not—"

"Yes, it is. Because if I was a virgin, we could have a relationship."

I stare at her. Is she right? If she was a virgin, would things be different?

Yes . . . and no. *Yes* because we'd both be beginners, which seems like a better foundation for a relationship. *No* because my own history would still be sick and rotten with what happened to me when I was twelve.

But that can't be part of our conversation.

"I don't mean it like that. I don't care that you're not a virgin. I don't care how many guys you've slept with." I take a breath. "Do you want the truth? Your experience is sexy. *You're* sexy. You're the sexiest fucking woman I've ever known."

Her eyes are searching mine like she's trying to figure me out.

"You said if I teach you about sex, that would mess with your whole gender role thing where the guy is supposed to have more experience than the girl."

"Well . . . yeah. Maybe that sounds old-fashioned but—"

"I don't know if old-fashioned is the word I'd use, but whatever. The point is that it sounds like we can't be together either way."

I'm not sure what's she's getting at.

"What do you mean?"

"Well, if we decide to be friends we won't be together. And if we decide to have sex, you're saying we *still* can't be together. Not romantically."

"Um . . ."

"So here's what I'm thinking. Since we can either *have* sex and not be in a relationship or *not* have sex and not be in a relationship, why not go for option number one?"

I'm sure there's a flaw in this logic.

"But if we do that . . . if we have sex . . . then we won't be friends. I mean, how can you be friends with someone you're sleeping with?"

She levels those gray eyes at me. "We're not friends now, Daniel. We want each other too much. You think that'll go away?"

I look back at her. Her cheeks are still flushed and her lips are still swollen, and for the first time I notice her nipples through her T-shirt.

"No," I say after a moment. "I don't think that'll go away."

Our hands are still clasped together. Now Tamsin pulls hers away and slides off the stage. Her boots don't have heels, and the top of her head barely clears my chest.

"I have a suggestion," she says, her head tilted back as she looks at me. "Do you want to hear it?"

She's smiling, and there's a wicked gleam in her eye.

"Okay."

"Let me be your teacher. Unless you're planning to stay a virgin the rest of your life, you'll have to figure this whole sex thing out at some point, right? So figure it out with me. No strings attached, no relationship necessary. Just sex."

There might be a guy somewhere who could resist that offer, made by the sexiest, sweetest, most beguiling girl in the universe, but I can't.

I'm still worried about my hang-ups and my past. But Tamsin's right. I've got to figure out a way past that shit sometime, and why not do it with the girl I've wanted from the moment I first saw her?

"Okay," I say.

She blinks. "Seriously?"

I feel like I've just stepped off the edge of a cliff.

"Yeah."

She lays her hands flat on my chest, and I wonder if she can feel my heart pounding.

"You won't regret this decision, Daniel Bowman. I'm going to give a whole new meaning to the phrase *sex ed.* Now, just to give me some background—you've obviously kissed girls before. I mean, no one can kiss like you do without experience."

At least she thinks I'm a good kisser.

"Yeah."

"And I remember our first Experiments in Drama class, when you revealed your favorite thing to do in bed with someone.

I swallow. "Yeah."

"Are you any good at it?"

An image floods my mind. Tamsin's on the stage again, lying on her back with her skirt up around her hips. But this time, I slide her panties off and go down on her.

"Very good," I say.

Her smile is the sexiest fucking thing I've ever seen.

"Damn. Okay. I'm assuming girls have gone down on you, too? And that you've gotten hand jobs?"

I tense up a little. If I tell her the answer is no, will she figure out something's wrong with me?

Maybe. But all the same, I'll tell her the truth.

"No," I say. "I've never gotten a hand job or a blow job."

I tense up even more, waiting for Tamsin to look at me like I'm a freak.

"Wait a sec," she says. "Are you telling me that you go down on girls but they don't go down on you?"

"Um. Yeah."

"How are you not the most popular guy on campus?"

I relax a little.

"Very funny," I say. "But girls think it's weird if you don't want them to reciprocate. And they think it's weird if you don't want to have sex."

"Okay, that's probably true. But you tell them why, don't you? I mean . . . I'm assuming it has something to do with religion."

I've never been more tempted to tell that lie.

"No. It's not because of religion. I've just never had a hand job or blow job. That's all."

I hope that's good enough.

It seems to be, because Tamsin's moving on to other things. "So," she says. "About coming over tonight . . ."

I shake my head. "No way. I've got an early class tomorrow. If we're really going to do this, I don't want there to be anything on my mind but you."

A smile curves up those incredible lips. "I like the sound of that."

I clear my throat. "I've got an away game this weekend, like I said. But after that we've got a bye week. No game." I pause. "I'm going to take you out next Saturday night."

She's still smiling. "I notice that you can still swing the alpha male vibe . . . in spite of your lack of sexual experience."

I know she's teasing, but something occurs to me. "Shit. I hope this goes without saying, but . . . I obviously don't have any expectations. I mean, if you change your mind about the whole sex thing, that's totally cool."

Her eyebrows go up. "I won't change my mind, Mr. Bowman. What about you?"

Given my history, changing my mind should be a distinct possibility. But as I gaze down into Tamsin's beautiful eyes, I know it's not.

"I won't change my mind."

"Then I guess it's a date."

She pulls back, and I miss her hands on my body like warmth on a winter day.

"I'll see you in class on Thursday," she says.

"See you then, Tamsin."

She smiles at me one more time, turns, and leaves the theater.

I'm left standing there, alone in the echoing silence.

I should be terrified, and I suppose I am.

But I'm also more excited for next Saturday than I've ever been for anything in my life.

CHAPTER SEVENTEEN

Tamsin

Ever since I met Rikki, I've trusted her. Over the last two years I've told her my hopes, my dreams, and every detail of my past. I've probably told her way more about myself than she ever wanted to know.

But I don't tell her that Daniel is a virgin.

I tell her he's taking me out again next Saturday night. I tell her I'm excited. But I don't tell her what he told me about his sexual experience . . . or lack of it.

I don't know how to explain what I feel when I think about that. It's a kind of tenderness. Protectiveness. It's like the other side of that melting feeling that happens in my chest whenever Daniel says something sweet and chivalrous.

He shared something personal with me, and I'm not going to tell anyone else.

We see each other in class on Thursday night, but we don't do a scene together. I'm grateful for that, because if we were on stage my feelings would show like a neon sign over my head. The few words we do exchange—*Hey, how's it going, not bad, how about you*—feel heavy and charged with things we're not saying.

I don't see him at all over the weekend, but I watch every minute of his away game on TV. Daniel plays for most of the third quarter. I honestly have no idea if he's good or not, but the way his butt looks in his uniform is definitely good.

I check in with Will, who tells me that Daniel made some excellent plays. I'm glad, because that gives me an excuse to DM him after the game.

Congratulations on the win. You did great. How are you feeling? It looked like you took a couple of hard hits.

After a moment, I send a second message.

By the way, here's my phone number if you want to text.

I attach my contact info and hit Send again.

As soon as I do, I regret it. Have I learned nothing from all my past relationships? Sounding overeager is a rookie mistake.

Not that this is a relationship, of course. More of a teacher-student thing.

But I still shouldn't have sent a message. Daniel is probably hanging out with his teammates. He probably won't even see this DM until tomorrow, which means

I've condemned myself to a night of checking for a response that won't come.

Rookie mistake, Tamsin.

Ding.

I sit straight up in bed, so suddenly that Rikki, writing an essay at her desk, looks up from her laptop.

"Something wrong?"

"No, everything's good."

I wait until she goes back to work. Then I open the text Daniel sent me.

I kept meaning to give you my number and I kept forgetting. Thanks for sending me yours. Thanks for the congrats, too. Can I admit something? I was hoping you were watching that game, because I was in for ten minutes and didn't do anything stupid.

For some reason, this message makes tears prick behind my eyelids. But I'm smiling as I answer it.

You were awesome, and I was very impressed in gender-normative fashion. Cue my girlish worship of your manliness on the football field.

I pause and read that over. Then I add,

But in all seriousness, you did a great job. And I'm glad you didn't break any bones or anything.

His response comes in less than a minute.

Me too. I want all my body parts intact when I take you out next Saturday.

My heart skips a beat, and I press a palm to my cheek to see if my skin is as warm as it feels.

It is.

When are you getting back to Hart?

I hope that doesn't sound too eager, or like I'm expecting to see him before class on Tuesday. But I'm less worried about that than I was a few minutes ago.

It's kind of nice to text a guy without parsing your words and worrying how he'll take them.

We're staying overnight and coming back tomorrow. What are you doing this weekend? Do you have a lot of work?

Medium. I've got a test on Wednesday and an essay due Friday, and I just found out the theater department is doing Romeo and Juliet in December. Auditions are next Sunday but I'm starting to prep now. Charlie is going for Romeo, so we're going to join forces and do a scene together.

You'll do great. But it's too bad they're not doing The Tempest. You could do a gender-bending thing and audition for Prospero.

I smile as I type my response.

I thought you said you didn't remember anything about The Tempest. How did you know the speech I did was Prospero?

I read the play on the bus this morning.

He did?

You did?

Yep. It's pretty good. I like that thing Ferdinand says to Miranda in Act III.

I'm about to ask which thing he means when a second text comes.

Hear my soul speak. The very instant that I saw you, did my heart fly to your service.

I stare at my phone. That's one of the most romantic lines in Shakespeare, which is a really high bar.

My heart is pounding. It takes a few tries for me to type a response.

That's a good line. I'm glad you enjoyed the play. We should go see it sometime.

I'd like that.

My heart is still pounding. What I'm feeling now is too intense. I need to end the conversation before I say too much.

I'd better get started on my essay. Rikki's at her desk working like a dog and she's making me feel guilty.

Have a good night, Tamsin.

You too.

I'll see you Tuesday.

See you then.

I put the phone down on my bed. Then, because I'm already tempted to text him again, I slide it under the pillow and out of sight.

Then I lean over, grab my *Complete Works of William Shakespeare* from the bookcase beside my bed, and open to *The Tempest.*

I read Act III, Scene 1, about twenty times.

* * *

I don't know how I get through the next week.

I'm so focused on Saturday night it's hard to concentrate on anything else. I manage somehow, but it feels like I've had a few drinks and I'm keeping it together just enough to pass for sober.

Daniel and I are almost formal with each other during Experiments in Drama. Izzy doesn't say anything about it on Tuesday, but she asks what the hell is wrong with me as we're leaving class Thursday night.

"What do you mean?"

"You can hardly even look at Daniel. Don't you guys have a date on Saturday? If you don't like him, you shouldn't go out with him. I don't care how hot he is."

That makes me smile. "He is pretty hot, isn't he."

"Yeah. But if you don't enjoy being with him you shouldn't go out with him. And anyway, a guy that good-looking has to be a serious player. I was sort of hoping you'd end your celibate period with someone you could really fall in love with. You deserve that."

As I look over at Izzy, I'm suddenly filled with affection. I stop in the middle of the quad and throw my arms around her.

"Argh! Cut it out."

"I won't cut it out," I say, squeezing her harder. "You're such a good friend."

"Stop hugging me! You know I'm not a hugger."

"Yes, I know. But I'm working to change that one hug at a time."

* * *

Saturday night finally comes. I'm so keyed up Rikki says she can't stand it anymore, and she leaves to go to the library.

Now I'm alone with twenty minutes until Daniel gets here. I put on Tom Waits, but I decide that's too obvious. Then I put on Jeremy Enigk because he's Christian, amazing, and also obscure enough that Daniel might not have heard of him.

I look at myself in the mirror for what has to be the ten thousandth time. I really did it up tonight—a vintage green satin cocktail dress with a black leather belt. And because thinking about Daniel makes me feel very, very naughty, I'm also wearing thigh-high fishnet stockings and black spike heels.

My hair is loose and I've got on dangly green earrings. No necklace or other jewelry, but I'm wearing fingerless fishnet gloves to match my stockings.

A knock on the door. My heart is all aflutter, which is a phrase I've never even thought before this moment.

I tell myself to get it together and open the door.

Daniel's wearing jeans and a plain black T-shirt. It's the first time I've seen him dressed so casually, and now I understand why.

If he walked around looking like this every day, he'd be too busy beating women off with a stick to get anything done.

"Wow," he says to me. "You look incredible."

"So do you."

Then we just stand there, staring at each other.

"I'm sorry," he says after a moment, his voice a little husky. "I got flowers for you but I forgot to bring them. I also can't remember the restaurant I'm taking you to. But I made a reservation, so if I look in my phone history I should be able to figure it out."

I start to smile. "Are you saying you can't think straight around me?"

"That's exactly what I'm saying."

"Well, join the club. It's a miracle I didn't fall through a manhole or get run over this week."

There's a foot of space between us, but it doesn't feel like air. It feels like something thick and luscious and honeyed.

There's no first move. He doesn't go in for a kiss, and neither do I.

It's more like spontaneous combustion.

Daniel spins us around, backing me up against the door he just closed. His hands are on either side of my head, his body caging me in.

His lips are everywhere. My hair, my cheeks, my shoulders, my neck, and finally my mouth again.

I've been craving the taste of him for so long. But now that we're finally kissing, it's not enough. I'm ravenous.

He seems to feel the same. He bites my lower lip and then licks where he bit, and I feel a whimper come from deep in my throat.

When he pulls back, his eyes are wild.

I feel as wild as he looks. I feel half savage, and the thought of doing anything but this is impossible.

"Daniel," I manage to say. "I really, really appreciate the work you put into planning our date. But I'm not hungry and I don't want to go anywhere. I don't want to leave this room. I just want to—"

He cuts me off with another kiss. This one is deep and wet and carnal, his tongue thrusting against mine.

It doesn't seem possible that I could come from just a kiss, but damn, my panties are already wet.

And then, just as I'm feeling frantic, he slows down.

The stroke of his tongue turns deliberate and sensual. His hands were braced against the door, but now they slide into my hair.

My scalp prickles so intensely it feels like an electric shock.

His hands move to my shoulders. He breaks our kiss, but only so he can kiss me again.

And again.

His hands drift up a little, and now his thumbs are caressing my throat.

The skin there is so sensitive. His hands, strong and powerful, remind me how vulnerable I am. How open.

And all I want to do is open more.

I arch my neck back, and he kisses the hollow above my collar bone. Then he drags his mouth up to the hollow beneath my jaw.

Then, suddenly, his hands and his mouth are gone. My eyes flutter open as he falls to his knees in front of me.

His gaze locks with mine. His head is level with my breasts, and it's obvious that this fact has not escaped him.

His hands circle my waist. Then they slide up over the green satin covering my ribcage.

I can't seem to catch my breath. If I don't get some oxygen soon I—

A pause. A beat. And then, so slowly I almost pass out, his hands move to cover my breasts.

I'm not wearing a bra. There's only one layer of material between his palms and my bare skin.

I've been with a lot of guys. Twenty-three, to be exact. And for most of them, my breasts were a brief stopover on the way to Sextown.

Not for Daniel.

He's looking. He's touching. He's practically worshipping.

His thumbs move over my nipples, and I didn't know it was physically possible for them to get any harder. They're doing their best to poke through my dress, and if Daniel keeps stroking them like that it may happen.

Finally he releases my nipples from their sweet torture, but only so he can hook his thumbs under my spaghetti straps and slide them off my shoulders. He pulls my bodice down, slowly, until I'm naked from the waist up.

"Tamsin," he whispers.

Then he leans forward and takes my right breast in his mouth.

Oh, God.

My hands have to go somewhere, and they find their way to the back of Daniel's head. I hold him close as he lashes my nipple with his tongue again and again and again.

He pulls back and blows cool air on my skin, and I shiver all over. Then he covers my right breast with his warm palm and puts his mouth on my left nipple.

Oh, *God.*

When he bites down, a bolt of electricity shoots straight between my legs.

My hands slide through his hair as he pulls back again. This time he's got his sights set on my belt. He unfastens it, slowly, and lets it drop to the floor.

Then his hands go to my waist. He tugs my dress down over my hips, and in the next second I'm standing in a puddle of green satin.

I'm breathing like I've been running. My knees are weak. And Daniel is looking at me like I'm the most beautiful woman he's ever seen.

His gaze travels from my patent-leather heels to my thigh-high fishnets, and comes to rest on my black mesh panties.

"Holy fuck."

My breath comes out in a whoosh.

"That sounds pretty blasphemous, Bowman."

He circles my ankles and then draws his hands up, slowly, to my thighs. He stops at the top of my fishnets, his thumbs stroking the bare skin above my stockings and below my panties.

"How do these stay up?" he asks softly.

"The same way I'm standing right now," I tell him, my voice trembling. "Sheer willpower."

He looks up, and when our eyes meet it's like the earth cracking.

"You're having trouble staying on your feet?"

I nod.

"We can't have that."

And before I know what's happening, he's got one arm behind my knees and the other around my shoulders and he's carrying me toward the bed.

Judging by the effort it takes him, I weigh about as much as a kitten.

I lock my arms around his neck and whisper in his ear, "I'm kind of digging this whole gender role thing."

Then I take his earlobe between my teeth and bite down.

He gasps, and his hold on me tightens. Then the two of us are falling, tumbling, plummeting onto my bed in a tangle of arms and legs and my puffy blue comforter.

Somehow we end up in the perfect position. I'm on my back and he's above me, his hips cradled between my thighs. My breasts are crushed beneath his chest, my hands are gripping his shoulders, and we're kissing, kissing, kissing like we'll never stop.

His body on mine. His mouth on my mouth. Our lips, our teeth, our tongues, our breath. Then he pulls back, breaking the kiss, but only so he can bite my neck.

I cry out, arching my head back on the pillow.

I make more sounds but nothing resembling words. He's kissing his way down my throat to my breasts and I wish he'd bite me again.

I wish he'd leave a mark I could carry forever.

He lavishes attention on my breasts and I feel like a goddess. I slide my hands into his hair, gripping with my fingers until I must be hurting him.

He doesn't complain.

Then he moves lower, kissing down my breastbone to my stomach.

My muscles tense in anticipation. My whole body is quivering.

He raises his head and looks at me. His eyes are dark and intense and so fucking sexy I almost come.

"Is it weird that I want you to keep your shoes and stockings on?"

I've never felt so lustful and so full of affection at the same time.

"I dressed like this to turn you on. Are you telling me it worked?"

"You could have worn full body armor and I'd be turned on. But yeah, it worked. I'm going to be fantasizing about you in fishnets for the rest of my life."

This boy is killing me.

"I'll make a deal with you. I'll keep my shoes and stockings on if you take some stuff off."

He tenses up a little, and I remind myself of all the things he hasn't done yet. The things I hope we do tonight.

After a moment he asks, "How much do you want me to take off?"

"As much as you want."

He hesitates another moment. Then he kicks off his shoes, letting them drop to the floor, and pulls off his T-shirt.

I raise myself up on my elbows. He's on his knees now, between my legs, and his bare chest looks like something out of a Playgirl calendar.

"You're making my mouth water," I tell him.

The hint of tension from before is gone.

"Right back at you," he says.

Then he grabs my panties and pulls them down and off.

I've never been with a guy who looks at my pussy like this—like it's the most delicious thing on the menu. But from this moment forward, I never want to be with a guy who doesn't.

Daniel settles down between my legs and puts his hands on my hips.

I'm so wet already. So aroused. Watching Daniel is almost too much, and I squeeze my eyes shut so I don't come just from looking at him.

That's when I feel his tongue.

My fingers curl into the comforter. He hooks his arms under my knees and urges my legs apart—farther apart than he really needs them to be. Being spread open like this makes me feel deliciously helpless, and a rush of heat ignites my entire body.

His mouth tortures and worships me at the same time. I start to writhe as the tension ratchets up, but his grip is like iron. I'm a prisoner to desire and all I can do is let Daniel carry me to the peak, higher and higher until—

When the explosion comes I cry out. He took me so high I fall forever, floating on clouds of bliss.

Coming down takes an eternity, but it's not long enough. The sweetness of this moment is so intense I can't move. I can't speak. All I can do is ride the aftershocks as they ripple through me, tingling with voluptuous electricity.

Daniel is kissing his way up my body. The pressure of his lips is soothing and thrilling at the same time, and every kiss feels like a drop of pure joy.

When he settles down beside me, I open my eyes and look at him. His head is pillowed on his bent arm and his dark blue eyes gaze into mine. He reaches out, drawing the backs of his knuckles down my cheek.

"God, you look so beautiful right now."

His voice is deep and husky, and sexy enough to melt any parts of me that aren't already melted.

"It's the post-orgasmic glow," I tell him. "It makes every girl look good." I pause. "Speaking of which, you weren't kidding, were you?"

"Kidding about what?"

"You are very, very good at that."

He smiles. "Actually, I've never been that good before."

"What made this different?"

"The person I was with."

That sweet sensation behind my breastbone is back. I shift onto my side to face him, pillowing my head on my arm to mirror his position.

"I need a minute to recover from my shattering orgasm. But then I'd like to return the favor."

He goes still. The tension is subtle, but I'm so attuned to him right now I feel it.

"Daniel," I say softly, trying to feel my way through something I don't understand. "I don't want to do anything you don't want to do. But when we were kissing, I could feel how hard you were. Can you tell me what's going on? I really, really want to go down on you, and it seems like you want that too. Or at least your body does. Am I wrong?"

The muscles in his throat jump as he swallows.

"No. You're not wrong."

"But?" I prompt after a moment.

Another beat goes by. Then: "What we just did was so fucking perfect. I want to wallow in that for a while without worrying about my hang-ups."

I still don't understand, and I'm worried about saying the wrong thing.

"Hang-ups?"

He rolls onto his back and stares up at the ceiling. "Well, I must have some hang-ups, right? I'm a twenty-year-old guy who's never had a blow job. I'm surprised you don't think I'm a freak."

"And I'm a twenty-year-old girl who's slept with twenty-three people. I'm surprised you don't think I'm a slut."

He turns his head to look at me again. "It's not the same thing."

"Isn't it? Aren't we talking about judging people for their sexual experience, whether it's too much or too little or whatever stupid-ass thing someone might say?"

He smiles at that. Then he turns onto his side again, facing me, and this time he reaches out to cup the side of my face.

I didn't know how much I missed his touch until I felt it again.

"Maybe," he says. "And you were right about something else. I really, really want you to go down on me. But not right now. You know what I'd like to do right now?"

His hand slides into my hair, and I close my eyes.

"What?"

"I'd like to fall asleep with you in my arms. And then, in the morning, I'd like to revisit the whole you-going-down-on-me thing."

I'm leaning into his caress like a cat. "That sounds fair. I think I could be down with that plan." I pause, opening my eyes. "Would you be comfortable taking your jeans off? You could leave your boxers on," I add quickly.

He smiles again. "Yeah. I think I'd be comfortable with that."

He sheds his jeans, and while he does I kick off my shoes and peel off my stockings. Fishnets are all very well for sexy times, but for cuddling and sleeping they're not so comfortable.

I'm totally naked now while Daniel is in navy blue boxers. As he pulls me into his arms, the feel of his strong muscles and warm bare skin wakes up my hormones.

But Daniel is being careful to avoid any contact below the waist, and my lady parts have had plenty of fun for one evening. I can wait until tomorrow morning for more.

CHAPTER EIGHTEEN

Tamsin

I don't remember falling asleep. I remember lying in Daniel's arms and smelling the clean male scent of him, and feeling safe and protected and cherished.

The next thing I know, a shaft of sunlight hits my face and I'm blinking.

I'm still in Daniel's arms, and I don't ever want to move.

He's still asleep. His breathing is deep, his expression relaxed.

And God, he's handsome.

I replay everything that happened last night, from the incredible kiss up against my door to the best orgasm I've ever had. Daniel made me feel so good the echoes are still reverberating in my body.

I'm in a golden haze of sunlight and pleasure. I'm also more awake with every passing second, and the only thing I can think about is making Daniel feel the way I did last night.

If he's like most guys, he's halfway hard right now. All I have to do is slide down his body, lower his boxers and—

Daniel surges up with a gasp. His body spasms, his legs jerking toward his chest, and one of his knees cracks me on the chin.

I tumble off the bed and land on my butt.

The pain in my face is so intense I wonder for a second if I've fractured something.

I lie where I fell, stunned. And then Daniel is there, kneeling in front of me, his expression frantic.

"Holy shit, I'm so sorry. Where did I hit you? My God, Tamsin, I'm so sorry."

My hand goes to my chin. Daniel's hands follow and he feels around gently.

"Can you open your mouth? Can you move your jaw from side to side?"

I do.

"Can you talk?"

"I . . ." I pause and try again. "Yes, I can talk."

My eyes well up with tears.

It's not just the pain. It's the shock.

I'm staring at Daniel, and he looks like he got hit in the face too.

"Ice," he says. "I need to get you some ice. Is there a kitchen on this floor?"

I nod, and the movement is enough to make my tears overflow. "Down the hall to the left."

He doesn't even stop to put on his jeans. He goes out into the hall in his boxers.

I'm still naked. I stumble to my feet and go over to the bureau, and by the time Daniel comes back I'm in a T-shirt and sweatpants and sitting on the edge of my bed.

He's got some ice cubes in a Ziploc bag. He comes over and kneels down in front of me, and when he holds the ice to my face I take it from him.

The bag is wet and cold and my face hurts so much and Daniel looks miserable and everything is terrible.

"Tamsin, I'm so sorry."

"It's my fault," I mumble. "I should have waited until you were awake before I—"

"It's not your fault. You were being sexy and amazing because you *are* sexy and amazing. I'm the one who's fucked up. I should never have tried this. It was a mistake, and I—" He shakes his head. "It was a mistake."

My heart squeezes in my chest.

A mistake. The best night of my life, a mistake.

I lower the ice bag. "So on top of kicking me in the head, you're also breaking up with me?"

When I hear my own words, I hate myself.

"Not that we were going out," I add bitterly. "I mean, we can't break up if we're not going out."

"Tamsin—"

The tears are flowing freely, and I use my free hand to wipe them away.

"That's what I said, right? No strings, no relationship necessary. Just sex. A teacher-student thing." My chin and jaw are throbbing and it hurts to talk. "I guess I'm a really sucky teacher, huh?"

Daniel is still on his knees. "Tamsin. Tamsin. You're an amazing teacher. The problem is, you shouldn't have to teach me anything. I'm the one who's a fucked-up freak."

He's not a freak. But maybe he does need some help to figure out what's going on.

"Have you ever thought about seeing a therapist?"

At this point, I'm just trying to keep him here. To keep him talking to me. Because once our conversation is over, so is our relationship.

Not that we're in a relationship, of course.

But the more we talk, the more I feel him pulling away.

"I'm not interested in therapy." He looks away from me, frowning. "I have to go."

I open my mouth to say something else. Anything else.

But then I slump down, my shoulders sagging. What's the use? More importantly, where is my pride? If Daniel wants to go, he should go.

"Okay," I say.

Daniel was starting to get to his feet. Now he stops and kneels down again, taking my free hand in both of his.

"I'm sorry this didn't work out. I'm sorry I hurt you. Like, literally hurt you. But you should know it's a lot worse for me than it is for you."

Last time I checked, I was the one with the bruised face and on the receiving end of the breakup.

Not that we were ever a couple.

"Yeah?" I say. "Why's that?"

"Because I'm in love with you."

My heart flies out of my body.

Daniel looks at me for a moment, his dark blue eyes burning into mine. Then he gets up, goes around to the other side of the bed, and starts to put on his clothes.

I turn my head to watch him, holding the bag of ice to my face again. Neither of us says a word.

Once he's dressed, he walks to the door. He stops with his hand on the knob and turns to look at me.

"Goodbye, Tamsin."

And then he's gone.

* * *

I'm sitting exactly where I was when Daniel left. I don't know how much time has gone by, but all the ice in my Ziploc bag has melted.

There's a knock on the door. Before I can wonder if it's Daniel, I hear Rikki's voice.

"Is everyone decent? Can I come in?"

"Yes." My voice comes out as a kind of croak, and I try again. "Yeah, it's cool. Come in."

Rikki opens the door.

"So how did it go with Daniel? Are you guys—" She stops. "What the hell happened to your face?"

I shake my head. "It's a long story."

Rikki crosses the room and plops down next to me on the bed.

"I've got time and you've got bruises. Start talking."

And so I tell her everything.

Rikki's a really good listener, and she doesn't say a word until I'm done. When I get to the part where Daniel said he's in love with me, though, her eyes get big.

"Wow," she says.

"I know."

"I mean, *wow.*"

"I know."

"What are you going to do?"

I scoot back on the bed so I'm sitting with my back against the wall.

"You're supposed to tell me. The point of going through this story was so you could give me sage advice."

Rikki shakes her head slowly.

"I've got nothing. On the one hand, Daniel is a good guy and he had the good taste to fall in love with you. But on the other hand, he's got some issues and he said you can't be together. This seems like a really high maintenance situation and I know you wanted to focus on your classes and acting this semester."

"You're right," I say.

Yet even as I acknowledge it, the tears start flowing down my cheeks again.

Rikki gets off the bed. Then she sits down again, right next to me this time, and puts an arm around my shoulders.

"What are you thinking?" she asks softly. "What are you thinking right now?"

"I'm thinking . . . I'm thinking . . ." I take a deep breath. "I don't know what I'm thinking."

"What are you feeling?"

As soon as she asks me that, I know.

"I'm in love with him. I'm in love with Daniel Bowman."

Then I put my head on Rikki's shoulder and sob.

* * *

It's a day to do nothing. It's a day to lie in bed and lick my wounds, the literal ones and the figurative ones. And since it's Sunday, I ought to be able to do exactly that.

But in a cruel move by the universe, the audition for *Romeo and Juliet* is this afternoon. My heart is in shreds and I look like I've been in a boxing match, and I have to go and pretend to be a pure, innocent thirteen-year-old experiencing first love.

I do have a few hours to wallow in my misery, and Rikki makes the most of them. She brings me tea and hot buttered toast, she fluffs my pillows and tucks my comforter around me, and she makes me take Advil. She also plays Yahtzee with me until it's time to get ready.

It's a good thing I own stage makeup, because I need it to cover up the spectacular bruise on the right side of my chin and jaw. I go simple on everything else, figuring that's right for Juliet, and by the time Charlie comes by I'm ready to go.

Rikki wishes us luck and we head out.

Charlie and I go through our scene as we cross the quad to the theater.

"I hope you do better when we're on stage," is his encouraging response.

"I'm sorry. I'm distracted right now, but I'll get over it. I promise I won't let you down."

Now I have to keep that promise. Not just for Charlie, but for myself, too. I love acting, I love Shakespeare, and I want to play Juliet in this production.

There's a crowd of theater students backstage when we get there, waiting to be called. Charlie and I head for one of the dressing rooms and find Izzy there.

"I thought you weren't going to audition for this," Charlie says.

"I changed my mind. I've been thinking about trying comic roles, and I figured the Nurse would be a move in that direction. I'm going to give it a shot, anyway." She puts her tote bag on the makeup counter and fishes around in it. "Plus, I brought something for Tamsin to wear."

"We're not doing costumes."

"I know. This is just an accessory."

She pulls out a blue velvet jewelry bag and hands it to me.

I turn it upside down over my palm, and a net of crystals spills out.

The crystals have been threaded onto thin black wire. Izzy picks it up, holds the edges between her thumbs and forefingers, and lays it on my head like a little cap.

When I look into the mirror, the black wire disappears against my hair. All I see are the crystals, sparkling like stars in the night sky.

"Oh, Izzy. It's beautiful."

She smiles at me in the mirror. "I know, right? My cousin had this whole *Romeo and Juliet* theme at her wedding, and all the bridesmaids wore these. They're actually called Juliet caps."

"A *Romeo and Juliet* themed wedding? Did the bride and groom kill themselves at the end?"

Izzy laughs. "That's exactly what I said to my mom when we were getting ready. She told me to shut up and be polite."

I reach up and touch one of the crystals. "It's too nice to wear at an audition. I'm worried something will happen to it."

Izzy shakes her head. "It's not valuable. It's really just fancy costume jewelry. But it looks beautiful on you, and you should wear it."

"Okay, you've convinced me."

Charlie grins. "She didn't have to work too hard, huh?"

I stick my tongue out at him. "Have you checked the schedule? When are we up?"

"About ten minutes."

Izzy looks at her watch. "I've got almost an hour to wait. I think I'll go to the kiss-and-cry."

That's what we call the back of the house on audition days. Friends who've come to support you sit there, and once your scene is over you join them to grouse about how bad you were and let them contradict you.

"Who's out there today?" I ask. "I know Claire and Rikki can't come—they're both working shifts at the library."

"Julia said she'd stop by. And I saw Daniel on my way in."

I blink.

"You saw . . . Daniel?"

"Yes."

"Daniel Bowman?"

"Yes."

"From Experiments in Drama?"

Izzy stares at me. "Yes, Tamsin. Daniel Bowman from Experiments in Drama. Also known as Daniel Bowman, the guy you've gone on two dates with. I assumed he was here because of you. Is everything okay with you guys?"

She and Charlie are both staring at me, and I hope the heavy foundation I'm wearing conceals my blush as well as it conceals my bruise.

"I didn't know he'd be here. I'm just surprised, that's all." I grab Charlie's hand and pull him to the door. "We should get up there."

I told Charlie I wouldn't let him down. But as we're waiting in the wings for the stage manager to call our names, my heart is pounding and I'm not thinking about our audition at all.

I peep around the edge of the curtain to look out into the audience. And there, sitting with the other students in the kiss-and-cry, is Daniel.

Izzy was right. He's here.

There are two Mercutios to go before Charlie and I are up. I pull out my phone and start to type.

What are you doing here?

His response comes pretty quickly.

You're an amazing actress, you deserve this role, and I'm here to support you.

I stare down at my screen for a good ten seconds. It's dark backstage, and my glowing phone makes a little halo of light as I stand between black velvet curtains.

Finally I type,

I'm glad you came. Will you meet me after the audition?

His reply comes immediately.

Yes.

I press the phone to my heart for a few seconds. He's here at my audition. He wants to talk afterward.

The world has gone from pit of misery to glorious possibility in the space of an instant.

When the stage manager calls my name and Charlie's, I go out onstage feeling like a young woman who can't wait to meet the man she loves.

In other words, I feel exactly like Juliet. And when Charlie speaks his first words as Romeo, it's not his face I see.

It's Daniel's.

CHAPTER NINETEEN

Daniel

I can't let go of my phone.

Tamsin doesn't hate me. I haven't completely fucked things up.

After I left her dorm this morning, I went to church. I was sick of myself, so I tried not to think of myself at all, but only of God.

There's a part of the liturgy called Prayers of the People. The congregation kneels down and we pray for the Church, for the world, for the nation, for those who are sick and those who have died.

There's something about praying for other people that puts your own problems in perspective. It's not that they go away. But you remember that suffering is part of the human condition, and that it's our job to help each other and comfort each other.

After church, I took a long walk. I thought about Tamsin. And I decided that she's someone I want in my life, no matter what.

Yeah, it's complicated. We can't be a couple, but I'm in love with her. I want her so much it's hard to think about anything else when I'm around her.

I don't blame myself for that. There's nothing wrong with what I feel for Tamsin—only with letting those feelings hurt her.

Sure, I wish we could have a relationship. But how much more evidence do I need that I'm not ready for that?

The reality is, I'm fucked up. But I don't have to let that affect Tamsin. I can be her friend, which is what I should have been all along. It was my own selfishness that screwed things up.

Then, as I was walking across campus, I saw a poster for the *Romeo and Juliet* audition.

Tamsin is auditioning for Juliet. A friend would go and support her.

So that's what I'm doing.

When her text comes, I tell myself just to be the friend that Tamsin deserves.

What I get back is more than *I* deserve.

She wants to talk. She's going to give me a chance to fix things.

Then, a few minutes later, she and Charlie come on stage.

She so beautiful my throat aches. She's wearing jeans and a white silk blouse, and there's something in her hair that sparkles like diamonds. I don't see a bruise on her chin, which either means I didn't hit her as hard as I thought or that she's wearing really heavy makeup.

I want to look at her forever, which should be my first clue that being just friends will be harder than I've admitted to myself. But it's not until she speaks that everything I've been thinking for the last few hours falls apart.

Charlie is gay. But as he and Tamsin declare their feelings, as they kiss with the passion of two teenagers in love, I feel a surge of jealousy that's stronger than poison.

I'm jealous of a gay man. Jealous of a fictional character. Jealous of anyone that Tamsin looks at that way, talks to that way, kisses that way.

Because eventually, it won't be another actor on stage. It'll be for real, and it will kill me.

The scene is almost done. Tamsin kisses Charlie again and says,

"My bounty is as boundless as the sea,
My love as deep. The more I give to thee,
The more I have, for both are infinite."

In that moment, Tamsin embodies Juliet. Her youth and innocence, her passion and sweetness, her generosity and radiant joy.

She deserves a Romeo, and someday she'll find one. But if I thought for one second I could be friends with her and watch that happen, I was fooling myself.

I stay until the end of her scene. I don't want to distract her by leaving. But as soon as she and Charlie exit the stage, I'm gone.

Tamsin texts me as I'm crossing the quad.

Where are you?

I keep walking as I text back.

I couldn't stay. I made a mistake. But you were incredible in that audition, and if you don't get the part it's a crime. I'll see you in class Tuesday night.

A few minutes go by with no response. Then,

Are you fucking kidding me?

I wince.

I'm sorry. I understand if you hate me.

As I send that text, I don't know what kind of response I expect to get back. But as the minutes tick by, I realize there won't be any response at all.

Which is probably just as well.

Not to mention what I deserve.

* * *

An hour later I'm in my room with the door shut, trying to concentrate on engineering problems. Trace and Beeker are out, and when I hear a knock at the front door I ignore it. I'm not expecting anyone, and if they're here to see one of my housemates they're out of luck anyway.

I've got to finish this project. It's due on Tuesday, and I've got football practice and a scrimmage tomorrow afternoon. But all I'm doing is staring at my computer screen when I hear a noise like tapping at my window.

At first I ignore it, figuring it's starting to rain or something. But then it comes again, louder this time, and it's definitely a triple knock. Tap-tap-tap.

I spin my desk chair around. And there, sitting on the tree branch outside my second story window, is Tamsin.

My brain literally can't compute what I'm seeing. For a long moment, all I can do is stare at her while she stares at me.

Then she leans forward and shouts at me through the glass.

"Are you going to let me in? It's not exactly comfortable out here."

I get to my feet in a daze, go over to the window, and raise the sash. Then I raise the screen, too, and reach a hand out to Tamsin.

It takes some scrambling, but after a minute she's standing in my room, dusting herself off.

She's wearing the jeans and white blouse from the audition, and that sparkling thing is still in her hair.

"What is that?" I ask stupidly.

She frowns. "What?"

"That thing in your hair. It looks like diamonds. I mean, I know it's not diamonds, obviously, but—"

"Oh, shit." She reaches up and touches her hair. "It's Izzy's Juliet cap. She leant it to me for the audition and I forgot to give it back to her." She glares at me. "I forgot because of *you.* Because you took off like a coward and I had to run around like a lunatic trying to figure out where you live. Andre finally dug up your address for me. And then you wouldn't answer your stupid door and I had to climb your stupid tree and now here I am, and you better believe you're going to talk to me."

She's breathing hard. Her eyes are glittering like the crystals in her hair. Her hands are on her hips and she looks pissed as hell.

She's the most beautiful girl I've ever seen. The most exciting, genuine, passionate person I've ever known. And there's only one thing I really want to do right now.

I close the space between us, put my hands on either side of her face, and kiss her.

I'm gentle, because I can see the bruise under her makeup and I can't stand to hurt her again. But Tamsin grabs my shirt and yanks me close, and suddenly the kiss isn't gentle at all.

Our tongues meet in a feverish tangle. My heart is pounding so hard the rush of blood is like a storm surge.

Her breasts are crushed against my chest, and I flash back to the memory of what she looks like naked.

The passion is so intense I forget myself, and when I break the kiss to drag my mouth along her jaw she yelps.

I jerk back, horrified. "Shit. I'm so sorry."

Tamsin is running her fingers over her chin and jaw, but she's smiling.

"It's okay. We need to talk before we make out again, anyway."

My mouth is still tingling from our kiss, and my pulse is racing. I take a deep breath and let it out slowly, and then I take a few steps back.

"Do you want to sit down?" I ask. My voice sounds rough, and I clear my throat.

Tamsin nods. "Okay."

There's the bed and the desk chair. Leaving the chair for Tamsin, I go over and sit on the edge of my bed.

Tamsin drags the chair closer and sits down facing me. We're only a foot or so apart, and I force myself not to reach for her hand. I don't want the insane physical chemistry between us to distract from whatever Tamsin needs to say.

It's starting to get dark out. I turn on the lamp beside my bed, and the glow makes the crystals in Tamsin's hair shimmer.

Her hands are folded in her lap, and I wonder if she's trying not to touch me, too.

She leans forward. "Tell me why you left the theater today. You said you'd meet me after the audition, and then you left."

It's hard to think straight looking into those big gray eyes.

"You were so good. God, you were amazing. But when you spoke those lines . . . and the way you looked at Charlie . . ." I shake my head. "I went there thinking we could be friends. I felt like shit about this morning and I wanted to fix it. But at the audition, I realized what being your friend would mean." I pause. "Someday you'll fall in love, and I'll have to watch it happen. I'll have to watch you look at a guy the way you looked at Charlie. And I won't be able to do it." I take a deep breath. "I can't be friends with you. I know that makes me a shitty, selfish person, but that's the way it is. I'm sorry."

For a moment she just looks at me. Then she says,

"Do you know why I was looking at Charlie like that?"

I shake my head.

"I was imagining he was you."

My heart clenches in my chest. "What?"

"I had to play a girl in love. So I thought about the guy I'm in love with."

I can't move. I can't say a fucking word. All I can do is stare at the girl I've fallen for—the girl who, against all odds and common sense, has fallen for me, too.

"But, here's the thing."

I knew there had to be a thing.

"We have to figure out the sex stuff. I mean, I'm cool with waiting if that's what you want to do. But I'm *not* cool with not talking about it. If we can't talk about it, we can't be together."

The possibility of being with Tamsin is a fantasy come to life. But even though I want this more than I've ever wanted anything, I don't think I can do what she's asking me.

"Of course," she goes on, "there is another option."

Another option?

"We could work through the problem right now."

I'm not sure what she means. "Work through the—"

"We could have sex. Like, tonight."

My mouth opens, but no sound comes out.

Tamsin's mouth is curved up in the wicked, sexy smile I love so much.

"Unfortunately, my skills are a little limited at the moment. I won't be able to go down on you until my jaw feels better. So that leaves plain old intercourse." She leans forward. "We could get it over with right here and now. Like ripping off a Band-Aid. What do you say, Daniel?"

What do I say?

I'm caught between two forces. One is my old baggage, weighing me down like an anchor. The other is my feeling for Tamsin, ripping through me like a tornado.

My hands tighten into fists.

Tamsin looks at me for a moment. Then she gets off her chair and kneels down in front of me.

"I'll tell you what," she says softly. "If you don't want to, that's okay. But if you do want to, you don't have to say anything. Just take this crystal thing out of my hair and put it somewhere. Izzy will kill me if anything happens to it."

I know what I want. I've never wanted anything as much as I want Tamsin right now. But I'm still stuck between the past and the present, and for a second I'm frozen.

Then I raise my hands. I slide them into Tamsin's hair and find the edges of the jeweled cap. I lift it, and then I lay it down on the bedside table.

When I look back at Tamsin, her eyes are like stars.

"Okay, then," she says. "There's just one thing you have to keep in mind."

I find my voice. "Just one?"

She smiles up at me. "This is going to be terrible."

I blink. "You mean . . . the sex?"

"Yep."

"It's going to be terrible?"

"Yep. Because it's your first time, and first times suck. But now that you know that, the pressure's off. Don't even think of this as sex. Think of it like a medical procedure."

I feel myself starting to relax. "A medical procedure."

"You got it. Now, the second time—and the third and the fourth and so on—will be a different story. But this time will totally suck. Awkward city. Embarrassing for both of us."

She stands up, her eyes still on mine. Then she grabs the hem of her blouse with both hands and pulls it up and off.

She's wearing a plain white cotton bra, and she looks like a Victoria's Secret model.

I remember exactly how her breasts feel against my palms. It's just natural human instinct when I reach out to touch her.

Tamsin takes a step back, that wicked smile curving up her lips again.

"Oh, no. No foreplay, no distractions. This isn't supposed to be fun, Bowman. We're getting down to business."

Then she kicks off her shoes, unzips her jeans, and shimmies out of them.

Her panties match her bra. Plain cotton, white, and sexier than underwear has any right to be.

God, her body is fucking perfect.

She points at me. "Now you. Pants and shirt, please."

It's the sexiest order I've ever followed.

"Yes ma'am," I murmur, pulling my T-shirt off and shedding my jeans.

Now I'm sitting on the edge of my bed in just my boxers.

I'm as hard as a rock.

"You have the finest body of any human being on the planet," she says.

I raise my eyebrows. "Nope. That would be you."

She smiles. "We're a couple of sexy beasts. Okay, Bowman. Are you ready for the next step?"

Amazingly enough, I am. Whatever it is.

"Yeah."

"All right, then."

She reaches behind her back, unhooks her bra, and lets it drop to the floor.

"I like this step," I say, and my voice sounds like a rusty gate.

She stands there a moment, letting me drink in the sight of her naked breasts. Her nipples are small and perfect, a dark rose color, and I remember exactly how they taste on my tongue.

Then she hooks her thumbs under the waistband of her panties. "Now you."

I grab the waistband of my boxers.

"We'll do this at the same time," she says. "Ready?"

"Ready."

We pull off our underwear together, and I'm completely naked with a girl for the first time in my life.

I honestly wasn't sure what would happen. I thought I might lose my erection.

But as Tamsin gazes down at me, I get harder than I was before.

I'm as hard as a fucking diamond.

Her eyes meet mine again.

"This is a pretty good start," she says, her voice husky.

"What—" My voice croaks, and I try again. "What now?"

"Now you lie back."

I do it, sliding up the bed so my head is against the pillows. I'm still hard. But as Tamsin gets on the bed with me, I'm not thinking about my cock.

"I want to go down on you."

Her eyebrows go up. "Trying to distract me?"

She's kneeling, and I only have a tantalizing glimpse of the dark triangle between her legs.

I shake my head. "I just want to taste you again."

She smiles slowly. "There'll be time for that later. All the time you want. But not now."

My heart is beating like a drum. "What happens now?"

"Now I touch you, and you do your best not to kick me in the head. Should we give it a try?"

All I can do is nod.

She reaches out slowly and carefully, and I almost wish she'd just grab me. Because now I have time to remember the beer my neighbor gave me eight years ago, and the way it felt lying on his couch with my head swimming, and the way it felt when he touched me.

I grit my teeth. This time I'm sure I'll go soft. But then Tamsin's small, soft hand closes around me, and I forget everything but her.

Oh, God.

The most beautiful girl on the planet is on my bed, naked, and her hand is around my cock.

This is the sexiest moment of my life.

For a moment we're both still. Then, slowly, Tamsin's hand starts to move.

"How does that feel?" she asks softly.

She expects me to say words? I open my mouth, but I can't speak.

There's that smile again. "If it's good, nod. If it's bad, shake your head."

I nod.

"Okay, then. Time for the next step."

She lets go of me, which is probably a good thing. I'm close to coming right now.

Then she lies down on her stomach to reach over the side of the bed, and the perfect curve of her naked ass almost sends me over the edge.

She grabs her jeans, takes her wallet out of her back pocket, and fishes out a square packet. Then she's back on her knees, facing me again.

"Can I put this on you? Or do you want to put it on yourself?"

I manage to speak this time.

"You."

"Okay."

She rips it open, and there's so much anticipation in the sound of foil tearing that I grip my quilt with both hands to keep from flying off the bed.

Tamsin is over me now, her knees straddling my thighs. She puts the condom against the tip of my erection and slowly, slowly, unrolls it until I'm covered.

Then she looks up to meet my eyes.

I've almost lost my capacity for rational thought, but one thing remains.

"You're not ready. I mean—I haven't done anything for you yet."

Tamsin reaches for my hand and guides it to her pussy. When I touch her, she's soaking wet.

I close my eyes. "Fuck."

"Yeah," Tamsin says, letting my hand go, and I open my eyes again.

She's smiling. "I've been ready for this since I came through your window. Now buckle up, because here we go."

Her knees are straddling my hips. She takes the base of my cock in her hand and guides me to her entrance, and she's so wet I can feel it through the condom.

Then, slowly, she sinks down.

My whole life has been leading up to this moment. Every song I've ever heard, every prayer I've ever spoken, every dream of love or paradise or ecstasy.

I'm trembling and I can't stop. I'm staring at Tamsin and she's staring at me, and the look in her eyes is something I want to see for the rest of my life.

Then she starts to move. Slow at first and then faster, and the pleasure spiraling up inside me is almost more than I can stand.

It can't be as good for Tamsin. It just can't. But then she leans forward with a sudden gasp, her hands flat on my chest.

"I'm going to come. Shit. I'm sorry."

Words don't make sense anymore.

"You're sorry because you're going to come?"

She pants as she speaks. "I wanted to make this last. But if I come it might set you off."

I look up at her for one second. The feelings rushing through me have ripped everything else away, and the only thing left is instinct.

I put my hands on her hips and flip us over.

She squeaks, her hands gripping my shoulders and her eyes huge. I'm still buried inside her, and as I look down at the woman beneath me, her beautiful face flushed and her lips parted, I make a sound I've never made in my life.

I growl.

And then I move, pulling out and thrusting in again, pulling out and thrusting in. Tamsin is so hot and wet and tight and perfect I growl again, and then she starts to moan.

Her eyes close as she arches her head back. Her body pulses around mine as she cries out my name, and that's what does it.

I shudder as I come. Tamsin's eyes are still closed but I keep mine open. I never want to see anything but her face, not ever again.

After a few seconds her eyes flutter open, and when she looks at me the whole world falls away.

There's only the two of us. We're wrapped in heat and sweetness, and there's a vibration in the air like the echo of thunder.

"Tamsin," I whisper.

"Daniel."

I press a kiss to her forehead.

"Say my name again."

"Daniel."

"Again."

"Daniel, Daniel, Daniel, Dan—"

I cut her off with a kiss.

Her arms slide around my neck and her mouth opens to mine. Our tongues meet and I want to kiss her forever. But I'm a lot bigger than Tamsin and I'm probably crushing her, so I break the kiss and start to pull back.

"Wait," she says, and I stop.

"What?"

"The condom. You want to grab it by the base before you pull out."

"Okay."

I do it like that and drop the used condom into the trash can beside the bed. When I roll back onto my side, facing Tamsin, I pull her into my arms.

"You lied to me," I murmur.

She nuzzles my chest.

"About what?"

Her voice is warm and sleepy and satisfied, and the sound of it is like a stroke against my skin.

"You said my first time would be terrible. You said it would totally suck."

"I said that?"

"You did."

She kisses the center of my chest. "So you're saying it *didn't* suck?"

"I am. In fact, I'm saying it was the best thing that ever happened to me."

I feel her smiling against my skin.

"It was all right for me, too," she says. "I mean, you know, it was okay."

I smack her bare butt, and she squeals. Then she pulls back and grins at me.

"This is literally the first time you've ever had sex and you're already into spanking?"

"Only with you, and only when you deserve it."

"Wow. That's a really good answer."

I know I should say something funny or snarky back. That's what we have going right now.

But I don't say something snarky.

"I love you."

Her eyes widen.

"I love you, too," she says, her voice trembling a little.

There's nothing I want to say after that. I just want to hold her, and feel her body against mine, and bask in this incredible glow.

Tamsin must feel the same way. Because when I pull her into my arms again, she doesn't say a word. She just nestles close and slides her arms around my waist.

This is the happiest I've ever been in my life.

CHAPTER TWENTY

Tamsin

I wake up in the middle of the night as hungry as a wolf. Which isn't really surprising, since I didn't eat much yesterday.

Daniel must have turned his bedside lamp off at some point, because it's pitch dark. His heavy arm is draped over my waist and I shift a little, trying to ease my way out from under without waking him up. There are three guys living in this house, and I figure there's got to be a kitchen downstairs with food in it.

Daniel's arm tightens around me as he nuzzles my ear.

"Where do you think you're going?"

The melting thing happens behind my breastbone. I would be totally down with making love again, but the fullness in my bladder and the emptiness in my stomach have to be addressed first.

"I have to pee. Also, I'm starving. Is there any food in the house?"

Daniel chuckles. "I guess the least I can do is feed you. We've got chips and pretzels and leftover Chinese and a bunch of frozen stuff. What are you in the mood for?"

"Anything but tofu."

He chuckles again. Then he turns on the bedside light, and when I see his naked body in all its glory I almost swoon.

Do women swoon in this day and age? If not, it's only because they don't see enough of Daniel Bowman naked.

"What?" Daniel asks, when he sees me staring.

"Nothing. Just . . . you're really pretty."

He grins as he swings his legs over the side of the bed.

"I'm not even the prettiest person in this room."

"Are you kidding? You're *way* better looking than I am. On any objective scale."

"You're out of your mind," he says as he pulls on his boxers and his jeans. "I'll go downstairs and grab us some food."

"A lot of food."

"A lot of food." He pauses at the door. "The bathroom's at the end of the hall. My housemates are probably home, so—"

"Don't worry. I'll put some clothes on."

"As long as you take them off again after we eat."

I'm still smiling as he closes the door behind him.

I put on my clothes, but before I go to the bathroom I do what every girl does alone in a guy's room. I walk around looking at everything.

A lot of football stuff, of course. Some photos of family and friends. A couple of music posters, including one of Tom Waits. Text books and some thriller novels I've never heard of and biographies of athletes.

And a Bible.

There are also a couple of framed prayers, one painted and one embroidered. I feel kind of taken aback when I see them. It's easy to forget that Daniel is religious, and my reaction to the Bible and the prayers makes me wonder if he was right about me all those weeks ago. Maybe I do have some kind of problem with religion.

Or maybe it's just that it's unfamiliar to me, and a little bit alien. After feeling so close to Daniel for the last few hours, it's probably good to have a reminder that we're still two very different people.

But that's true of any couple. Our football team's quarterback is Muslim, and he's dating a Jewish girl. If they can make that work, a Christian and an atheist can figure things out.

My bladder is starting to get insistent, and I go out into the hall to find the bathroom.

It's surprisingly clean for a house of just guys. There's toilet paper and soap and even a couple of hand towels. I resist the urge to open the medicine cabinet—reading a guy's book titles is cool, looking at his prescriptions is not—and go back out into the hall.

The rooms are all on one side, and the other side is a banister looking out over the first floor. I've only seen the second floor of Daniel's house—that's what happens when you come in through the bedroom window—and now I pause to look down.

The living room is pretty nice, and so is the part of the kitchen I can see from here. I'm about to go back into Daniel's room when I hear his voice floating up from the kitchen—along with a second voice I don't know. One of his housemates, I assume.

"What did I tell you about fucking a feminist?"

I freeze. And suddenly I remember something I've let myself forget—that one of Daniel's housemates trolls women on Twitter.

"Don't talk that way about Tamsin. I'm serious. You're crossing a line you don't want to cross."

"So she's *not* a feminist?"

"Not like the ones you make fun of. No."

Not like the ones he makes fun of? What the hell does that mean?

"You're fooling yourself, bro. Remember that question you asked me? Well, the shoe's on the other foot now. What are you going to do if she gets pregnant? What do you think *she'll* do?"

"I don't—"

"I'll tell you what she'll do. She'll get a fucking abortion. She'll go to those murderers at Planned Parenthood and kill that baby without a second thought. She's a goddam baby-killer."

My hands are squeezing the banister so hard my knuckles are white. This is who Daniel lives with? This is who his friends are?

"You're out of your mind, Trace. Tamsin would never get an abortion."

For a second I just stand there.

I don't decide anything consciously. I'm not even thinking, really. I just go down the stairs and through the doorway into the kitchen.

Daniel is leaning against the counter. Trace is sitting at the kitchen table. They both turn their heads when they hear me come in.

"Hi," I say. "I heard my name, so I thought I'd join the conversation."

Daniel looks upset. His housemate, on the other hand, looks pleased with himself. He also looks—and smells—like he's been drinking.

"The famous Tamsin," he says with a big grin. "It's an honor to meet you. So you picked my boy here to be number twenty-four, huh?"

It just goes to show that when you think things can't get worse, you're probably wrong.

But it might not have been Daniel who talked to him about me. It might have been Oscar or one of Oscar's friends.

I look at Daniel. "Did you tell this asshole how many guys I've slept with?"

He takes a step toward me. "No. Of course not."

Trace waves a hand. "Yeah, he did. He was drunk at the time, so he may not remember."

I relax a little. "Now I know you're lying. Daniel doesn't drink."

Trace looks at Daniel. "You want to set this bitch straight?"

Daniel gives him a look that would send any sober man running for the hills. "You call her that again and I'll rip you apart."

Trace grins again. "I apologize. Let me rephrase. Do you want to set this lady straight?"

I fold my arms. "Yes, Daniel, please do. Do you drink or don't you?"

His deer-in-the-headlights expression isn't exactly reassuring. "Not usually."

"Not *usually?*"

"I drank this one time. After our first date."

Trace nods. "That's right. He told me and Beeker—that's our other housemate, you should meet him sometime—that you'd slept with twenty-three guys. I guess

Danny boy was feeling a little insecure, since he's only slept with, what? Five girls?"

I'm trembling, and I hope to God they can't see it.

"Maybe you weren't lying about the drinking thing, but I know you're lying about this."

"Oh, yeah? I can't wait to hear why."

"Because Daniel—"

I stop.

Everything about this conversation is making me sick, but that doesn't mean I can tell this asshole Daniel's private business.

But Daniel can.

"Because he what?" Trace asks.

"He can tell you," I say.

Daniel looks at me, and then he looks at Trace.

"Tamsin is the first girl I ever slept with."

Trace stares at him for one second, and then he bursts out laughing.

"My God. I take back everything I ever said about you, Galahad. This is, hands down, the best scam a guy has ever pulled on a girl. You convinced her you were a virgin? That's fucking genius. You took all the pressure off yourself to do anything for her, and she was probably panting to do shit for you. I bet she worshipped your cock. And she felt all special, right? The first girl you ever slept with? God, you'd think a slut who's fucked twenty-three guys—sorry, twenty-four—wouldn't be such a gullible idiot."

Daniel's expression before was scary, but now it's more than scary.

It's murderous.

He's not looking at me, but I take a step back anyway.

"Stand up," Daniel says, and his voice is so cold a shiver runs down my spine.

"What's your problem, man? I'm proud of you."

Daniel crosses the space between them, grabs his T-shirt, and jerks him to his feet.

"Put up your fists."

Trace starts to laugh. "Put up my fists? What is this, a duel of honor? Over some stupid cunt?"

Daniel lets go of his shirt. Then he takes a step back.

The punch is so violent that Trace stumbles backward and falls. I see blood pouring from his nose and mouth, and then I turn and run.

I go upstairs because my shoes and wallet are still in Daniel's room. My hands are shaking but I manage to get the shoes on my feet and the wallet in my pocket.

I don't want to go downstairs again. I open the window and crawl out onto the tree limb, and then I climb down to the ground.

"Tamsin!"

It's Daniel, shouting at me from his open window.

I don't even look up at him. I take off, and it's only when I hear a thud and a curse that I turn around.

Daniel is on his ass at the base of the tree. I don't know if he fell all the way from the second floor or halfway down as he was climbing, and at the moment, I don't really care. But he's on his feet now and coming after me. Even though he's limping a little, he's a football player and I'm not, and if he chases me he'll catch me.

So I might as well get this over with now.

I stop and wait, and in a few seconds he's standing in front of me.

"You have to let me explain," he says.

"Sure thing. Go ahead."

He wasn't expecting that. He takes a moment to get himself together, and then he reaches for my hand.

I take a step back, and he doesn't try to touch me again.

"Trace is full of shit. Obviously. God, Tamsin, you have to know that."

"So you didn't tell him how many people I've slept with?"

That stops him short. He opens his mouth and closes it a couple times. Then he says,

"Okay, listen. I might have told him that. The night of our first date I was pissed at myself for fucking things up. I came home and drank for the first time since I've been at Hart. I'm honestly not sure exactly what I said. I was upset, and—"

"And you told your housemates about my sexual history."

He's quiet for a moment. Then,

"Maybe. But Trace was right about one thing. If I did, it was because I was insecure. That's on me, not you."

I nod. "Right. You were insecure because you've only slept with five people."

"No! Fuck. That's total bullshit. I've dated five girls since I came to Hart, but I didn't sleep with any of them. Maybe Trace assumed I did, but I didn't. I don't advertise the fact that I'm a virgin but I never lied about it, either. I haven't slept with any of the girls I dated and I never said I did."

I look at him for a moment, and it's so easy to remember the way his dark blue eyes made me feel just a few hours ago.

"You're not a virgin anymore," I say.

He swallows. "No."

"I'm glad I could help you out with that. Like Trace said, it made me feel very special."

He looks stricken. "Tamsin—"

"Shut up," I say, and he does.

I take a deep breath. "The fact that you told your housemates my sexual history sucks. The fact that Trace used that information to slut-shame me sucks, too. Of course, people have been trying to slut shame me since I was fifteen years old. I should be used to it by now." My hands are shaking, and I shove them in my pockets. "The fact that Trace thinks you lied about being a virgin as some kind of sex strategy also sucks, since I have no idea if it's true or not. But that isn't—"

"Tamsin. You can't think I'd—"

"Shut. Up."

He does.

"But that isn't the worst part. The worst part is that you're friends with someone like Trace. Someone who harasses women on Twitter and calls them bitches and sluts and cunts to their faces."

He doesn't say a word. He just looks at me like he's at his own execution, and I'm holding the axe.

"There's something else. You told Trace I'm not like the feminists he makes fun of, and you told him I would never get an abortion. What did you mean by that?"

"I just meant . . ." He stops. "I just meant . . ."

"What?"

"I just meant . . ."

I wait a few moments, but he doesn't finish the sentence.

"I think I know what you meant. I think you meant that I'm a reformed character now. Now that I've been sanctified by sleeping with you, I'll give up all my feminist ways. I'll go to church with you every Sunday. And I wouldn't dream of making a decision you don't agree with."

Then I turn and walk away. And this time, he doesn't try to follow.

CHAPTER TWENTY-ONE

Daniel

I go back to the house in a kind of daze. The first thing I see is Beeker standing in the kitchen doorway, watching Trace rinse the blood from his nose and mouth.

He turns when I come in. "What the fuck is going on? What the hell happened between you two?"

I have to fix things with Tamsin, and I will. But there's something else I have to do first.

"Trace is moving out."

Trace jerks upright and turns off the faucet.

"Fuck that. If anyone's moving out, it's you."

If Beeker hears the story and sides with Trace, I'd rather move out anyway.

"I'm fine either way. Let's tell Beeker what happened."

The amazing part is that Trace doesn't even disagree with my version of events. It's obvious he doesn't think there's anything wrong with what he said.

How could I have been friends with him for so long and not know what an asshole he is?

But that's not really how it's been. The truth is, I've always known what an asshole Trace is. It's not like he's ever hidden it.

It's just that I let it go.

Now I'm hearing Tamsin's voice in my head.

The worst part is that you're friends with someone like Trace. Someone who harasses women on Twitter and calls them bitches and sluts and cunts to their faces.

I've called out guys who use those words. But I've never stopped being someone's friend because of it.

Until now.

Beeker holds up a hand to interrupt Trace in a tirade I haven't been listening to. "Okay, that's enough. Trace, you're out."

Trace explodes, but I don't wait around to see that play out.

I should be glad I have one decent friend. But as I go upstairs to my room, I think about some of the things Beeker has said about women.

Even without calling anyone a slut, he's still managed to say some pretty shitty things.

I feel like I know what Beeker would say if I talked to him about that. He'd say he doesn't disrespect any of the women he actually knows. He'd say he just disrespects feminism in general. He'd say it's political, not personal.

Once I'm in my room, I go over to the open window. I start to close it but I sit down on the floor instead. I've got a throbbing headache and the cool air feels good on my face.

I'm starting to realize something.

I've been thinking I could have it both ways. I wanted to be part of the boy's club—or some version of it, anyway—and still be able to date a girl like Tamsin.

I wanted to be the good, decent guy who tells his friends not to call women sluts and not to make jokes about rape, but who could still be part of the club when the women aren't around and the jokes aren't too bad.

I thought I could keep the friends I know are assholes, and also be the kind of man Tamsin could fall in love with.

And that's a cowardly fucking way to live.

Tamsin is worth a million Traces, and I'll do whatever it takes to get her back. Including giving up the boy's club.

There are better guys to be friends with. Guys like Will and Andre. I've always assumed I don't have anything in common with them outside of football, because of my politics and my church. But maybe I've been wrong about that.

Maybe I've been wrong about a lot of things.

But kicking Trace out of the house was the easy part. My other problems with Tamsin run a lot deeper.

I haven't been honest with her.

Tamsin said she doesn't know if I lied to her about being a virgin. She said she has no idea if what Trace said is true or not. It kills me that she might believe Trace over me, but that's exactly what I deserve.

Because I haven't been honest with her.

I think about something she said.

Now that I've been sanctified by sleeping with you.

She said it sarcastically. But here's the thing.

I didn't sanctify her. She sanctified me.

I came to her broken, and she didn't laugh at me or reject me. She didn't decide I was too much trouble. She gave me a gift, and I didn't tell her what that gift meant to me.

I didn't trust her with the truth.

A chorus of bird song erupts outside, and I look out the window. Sometime in the last half hour the sky has gone from black to gray.

It's dawn.

I have a lab at eight. Should I muscle through and go to bed early tonight, or try to get a little sleep before class?

I glance over at my bed. The covers are rumpled, and the sight sends memories stabbing through me.

My body tightens. My heart squeezes in my chest.

I still don't know how to fix things with Tamsin. But I know I can't lose her.

I need to think. So I decide to do something I haven't done since I've been at Hart.

I decide to cut a class.

Cutting class to think sounds like something a snowflake liberal would do—not a hard-headed conservative engineering major. But I'm starting to believe those labels are fucking useless.

There's a park a few blocks over, and it's got miles of walking trails. I get dressed and grab my wallet from the bedside table, and that's when I see Tamsin's crystal thing, lying in a sparkling heap right where I put it last night.

I stare at it for a long time. Then I pick it up and put it in my pocket, and as I'm walking to the park I keep my hand closed around it.

CHAPTER TWENTY-TWO

Tamsin

I get back to the dorm late and wake Rikki up.

We talk for hours. She tells me to cut my Monday classes, which is pretty wild—she never ditches herself and she always gives me a hard time when I do.

But I don't do it. I don't get a lot out of my lectures today, but I go to them.

I talk to Izzy about her Juliet cap at dinner, and she tells me not to worry about it. Daniel might bring it to class tomorrow, and if he doesn't, she'll ask him to bring it next time. I won't have to talk to him.

I'm more grateful for my friends than I can ever express. Every time I think about them I start to cry.

But that's not the only thing making me cry.

I didn't cry last night when I was talking to Rikki. My anger was too hot and fierce then. Tonight, though, Rikki's at the library and I'm alone in our room. I can't focus on studying, but I'm afraid if I don't give myself something to do I'll start thinking about Daniel.

I'm not ready to think about Daniel.

I decide to do laundry. I gather all my stuff, including everything that's under the bed and on the floor of my closet.

That's when I find it: Daniel's red button-down shirt. I stuck it in my closet the night of our first date and forgot about it.

Now I pick it up and go sit on my bed.

It's just a regular men's shirt. Nothing special about it. But the thing is, it smells like him. Like soap and mint and something uniquely Daniel.

And before I know what's happening, my face is buried in that damn shirt and I'm sobbing like I'll never stop.

* * *

By the time I go to Experiments in Drama on Tuesday night, I'm feeling a little better. I'm not crying anymore, which is good, and I'm not mad anymore either. I feel sort of . . . I don't know. Not tired, exactly. More like I've been emptied out. Like so much emotion has been wrung out of me in the last few days I don't have any left.

There's been one piece of good news. The cast list is up, and Charlie and Izzy and I all got the parts we auditioned for in *Romeo and Juliet.* I'm genuinely excited to start work on the play.

Or at least, I will be once I get some feeling back in my heart.

I'm not looking forward to seeing Daniel, but I don't think he'll try to talk to me or anything. He texted once, this morning, to say he has Izzy's crystal cap and he'll bring it with him tonight.

Ok, I texted back.

Can we talk after class?

No.

And that was it.

Which is why I don't think he'll bother me tonight. I'm pretty sure he's gotten the message.

I get to the theater before him and sit between Charlie and Izzy. They know things went south between me and Daniel, and though I haven't told them as much as I've told Rikki, they're on my side and will play buffer if need be.

As students trickle in and Professor Washington makes her appearance, I tense up in spite of myself. Daniel usually comes five or ten minutes early, and now it's seven-thirty-two. Is he skipping class? A part of me hopes he does, but I know it would be better to get the first awkward sighting over with. Like ripping off a Band-Aid.

Oh God, wrong metaphor. That's the phrase I used to Daniel the night I crawled through his window.

And just like that I'm back in his bed, sharing the sweetest, most intense sexual experience of my life.

I hate thinking that Daniel might have lied to me about being a virgin. I hate thinking he might have lied about loving me.

I don't want to believe it, and in my heart I don't. My instincts tell me he was honest about those things.

But that, of course, is the whole problem. I don't know if I can trust my instincts anymore.

Then Daniel walks in the door, and all the warmth drains from my body.

I keep my head down, pretending to look at my phone. Charlie and Izzy shift a little closer to me, and that small comforting action makes me feel better.

I sense rather than see him walk up the stairs and past our row of seats. He usually sits up front, but tonight he goes to the back of the house.

And just like that, it's over. The first post-breakup encounter is in the books. He didn't try to talk to me, and I didn't burst into tears or recriminations. I call that a win.

But as Joan comes to the front of the stage and starts class, I don't feel like I've won anything.

"Okay, guys. Today we're going to dig a little deeper."

Great. Just what I *don't* feel like doing tonight.

"You might think dramatic skill starts with monologue and advances to dialogue. The more variables you add to an equation the more difficult it must be, right? But in acting, that's not necessarily so. In a dialogue with a scene partner, you can draw on the other person's energy. When you're doing a monologue, you have only yourself to rely on. So tonight, we're going to try some monologues. We've been talking about the intersection of the personal and the political, especially as it relates to our bodies, our beliefs, and our relationships. So tonight I want you to get as personal as you can. Tell us about a time someone else tried to define you. A time someone imposed on you—whatever that means to you."

She looks around the room for a moment and then zeroes in on me. "Tamsin, you've been very brave in your scene work so far. Why don't you start us off?"

Izzy grabs my arm and whispers, "You don't have to. I'll go up if you want."

I shake my head. "Thanks, but I'll be okay."

And as I walk up onto the stage—Joan put a wooden chair there for us to sit on—I realize it's true. It might take some time, but I'll be okay.

I sit down, take a deep breath, and look at the front row.

"My name is Tamsin Shay, and I'm Queen of the Sluts."

That gets a laugh.

I look up a little higher now, into the second row where Izzy and Charlie are.

"I say that for the same reason anyone says stuff about themselves. So that other people can't say it first. If you head them off at the pass, they don't have as much power to hurt you."

I shift a little on the chair, leaning forward and clasping my hands between my knees. I'm looking out at the whole audience now—except for the back row where Daniel is—but I know that if I need to focus on a particular face, I can look at Izzy.

"I got called a slut in high school even before I slept with anyone. I liked short skirts and high heels, and freshman year they called me Slutty Shay. So it was no big shock when they called me a slut sophomore year, after I did sleep with someone—or junior and senior year, when I slept with a lot of someones. I figured out when I was a virgin in high heels that it honestly doesn't matter what you do. If you're a girl who likes sex—or even just being sexy—someone's bound to call you a slut sooner or later. So why not own it, right?

"I did own it. I still do. But sometime in the last few days, I realized something."

For the first time, I glance up into the back row. Daniel's sitting absolutely still, his eyes fixed on my face. I look away again.

"I thought I was comfortable with who I am. Comfortable enough that no one could hurt me like I'd been hurt in high school. I thought the assholes had lost their power over me. And you know what? I was right. Their words can't hurt me anymore.

"But here's the thing. I still hurt. I still hurt, because somewhere along the line I let the shame inside me. It snuck through the door and wormed its way in.

"That's what I realized over the last few days. I've been telling myself all this time that no one has any right to judge me, and they don't. But that's not the problem. The problem is that I've been judging myself. I haven't forgiven myself for the choices I made when I was a teenager.

"Until I accept myself—until I forgive myself—nothing anyone else says or does will matter a damn. And that's where my real struggle is. Not out there, with them—but inside."

I get to my feet. As I cross the stage toward the stairs, there's silence in the house. Then, as I take my seat again, my classmates applaud.

"Thank you, Tamsin," Joan says. "I'm looking forward to seeing your work as Juliet. Now, who wants to go next?"

"I will."

My whole body tenses up at the sound of that voice.

As Daniel gets up and comes toward the stage, my heart starts to race. Goose bumps prickle every inch of my skin. And I wonder how long it will be before my body stops reacting to Daniel like he's the love of my life.

Stupid body.

He sits down on the wooden chair where I just was. He's wearing khaki pants and a navy blue button-down shirt. He rests his hands on his knees, and all I can think about is how those hands felt on my skin.

A few seconds go by and he doesn't start talking. A few seconds more, and it's the awkward moment when you're not sure if the actor is taking a dramatic pause or if he's forgotten a line. A few seconds after that, we're all wondering if Daniel has frozen up.

But now, finally, he begins.

"My dad died when I was a kid. It was a bad time, but we did the best we could. There wasn't a lot of money. My mom's a nurse and my dad was an ambulance driver, and most of his life insurance went to funeral expenses. We moved out of our house and into an apartment, and when one of our neighbors offered to babysit me and my sister so my mom could pick up extra shifts at the hospital, she was so grateful.

"Henry watched us on the weekends. He worked in a music store and played drums in a garage band, and he was the coolest guy I knew. When he told us he was moving away, I was really upset.

"A week before he left, my mom took my sister to some ballet thing. Henry invited me over so I wouldn't have to go with them. Then, when I got there, he offered me a beer.

"I was twelve years old, and I'd lost my dad. I had all these ideas about being the man of the family and no clue what that actually meant. Now here was this guy I looked up to, offering me a beer and treating me like a man.

"I chugged that beer like I'd seen people do in movies. Then I had another one. The next thing I knew, I was lying on Henry's couch with my head swimming, and he was touching me."

I freeze in horror.

Please, I think to myself. *Please, no.*

I don't even know what I'm pleading for. This happened in the past, and I can't go back in time and stop it.

"I didn't understand what was happening. He was touching me outside my clothes. Then he tugged down my sweatpants and pulled down my underwear and touched me again."

A wave of nausea goes through me. For a second I think I'll vomit right here in the theater. But I take a breath, and another one, and I manage to keep it together.

"I was still just lying there. I didn't do anything. I didn't jump up and run away. That's one of the reasons I thought what happened was my fault. For years I thought that.

"Of course, I tell myself now that Henry spent months making sure I trusted him. He knew I'd lost my dad. He knew I saw him as a surrogate father or whatever. And then he gave me alcohol.

"I tell myself all that now. It wasn't my fault, I tell myself now. But back then, all I knew was that I stayed there on Henry's couch and let him touch me.

"It was only when he took my hand and put it on his penis that I got up and ran away. I went into my apartment and locked the door. I went into my room and locked that door, too. I never saw Henry again. And I never told anyone what happened. Not my mom, not my minister, not anyone."

His eyes are on the floor. He's not looking at us. He's remembering the shame that bastard made him feel, and there's nothing I can do.

"There are guys who say that if a girl doesn't fight it can't be rape. They don't understand what it's like when someone you trust—or someone with more power than you—takes advantage. They blame the victim, and that's fucking evil. But even when I tell myself that, it still doesn't stop me from blaming myself."

He glances up for the first time, and his eyes meet mine.

"It's like Tamsin said. The hardest fight is always with ourselves. But, here's the thing."

He takes a deep breath and lets it out slowly.

"The hardest fight is with ourselves, but that doesn't mean we can stop fighting the assholes. Even if the assholes are our friends—or our ex-friends."

His eyes are still on mine. "I never told anyone I was molested. There are a lot of reasons for that, and most of them have to do with shame. I've known that for a long time. But what I didn't know—what I still don't know—is how much of my shame is because I'm a guy. Men aren't supposed to be victims. And so when we are, we don't talk about it."

He takes another breath. "The last couple of days, I've been wondering if the whole toxic masculinity thing isn't as stupid as I've always thought. And if women aren't the only ones hurt by it."

He stops talking, and there's dead silence in the theater. All around me the other students are just sitting there, frozen. But I'm not focused on any of them. I'm looking at Daniel, and he's looking at me.

Then he gets to his feet.

"Thanks for listening," he says.

He crosses the stage and goes down the steps. But instead of returning to his seat, he goes out the door.

There's still dead silence in the theater.

Then, after a moment, Izzy touches my shoulder.

"Go," she says, and I do.

CHAPTER TWENTY-THREE

Tamsin

Daniel's already gone by the time I get to the hall. I run to the exit and push through the door, and I don't see him right away. I panic, but then I catch sight of him across the quad, walking toward the library.

And now, suddenly, my frantic urgency disappears. I follow, but not fast enough to catch him.

A hundred different things are jumbled together in my mind. An image of Daniel at twelve years old, thinking he has to be the man of the family. An image of him in his neighbor's apartment being handed a beer.

I want to kill that piece of shit child molester. I want to destroy him. Tears well up in my eyes, and I wish for something else even more. I wish I could go back in time and protect the boy Daniel once was.

But that's not the only thing I'm thinking about.

I'm thinking about Daniel taking me to a vegan restaurant because he thought I'd like it. I'm thinking about him giving me his shirt to wear in the rain. I'm thinking about him texting me that quote from *The Tempest.*

I'm thinking about the way he went down on me with total abandon and looked at me like I was the most beautiful girl he'd ever seen.

And I'm thinking about the look in his eyes when he said he loved me, and the way it felt to say it back to him.

We're at the library now, and Daniel goes around to the back of the building. I'm moving faster now, catching up to him, and I'm close behind when he goes into a garden I've never noticed before. When he sits down on a bench under a maple tree, he sees me for the first time.

"Tamsin," he says, staring.

I feel eager and scared and shy all at once. I feel a thousand other things I can't even define.

But what I feel most of all is love.

"Daniel—"

"I'm glad you're here," he says, getting to his feet. "I wanted to tell you that Trace is gone. We kicked him out of the house. I wanted to tell you how sorry I am that he said all that shit to you. I wanted to tell you how much I—"

"Daniel," I say again, and he stops.

Now that I've gotten him to listen to me, I don't know what to say.

"Please don't," Daniel says suddenly.

I stare at him. "Don't what?"

"Don't tell me how sorry you are that I was molested."

And then, just like that, I'm crying.

"But I am sorry. Oh God, Daniel, I'm so sorry that happened to you."

He sinks down on the bench. His shoulders are slumped. I sit down beside him, wiping the tears from my face with the back of my hand.

"I don't want you to feel sorry for me."

"I don't."

"You just said you do."

"No. I said I'm sorry that happened to you. But I don't feel sorry for you. I don't pity you. You're my hero, Daniel."

The sun's down and it's almost nighttime. We're sitting in the gray shadows of dusk. But the lights are on in the library and the windows are right above us, and that's enough light for me to see that Daniel is shaken.

"You shouldn't say that."

"What?"

"You shouldn't call me your hero. Not after what I put you through at my house."

"You fixed it," I say. "That's what heroes do."

"But—"

"Daniel," I interrupt him, putting a hand on his shoulder.

He turns to face me, covering my hand with his, and a wave of heat and sweetness goes through me. And now, finally, I know what to say.

"I love you."

I feel a tremor run through him.

"I love you, too."

For a long moment we just stare at each other, and I could sit here like this for the rest of my life.

Then Daniel lifts my hand to his mouth and kisses it.

"Tamsin?"

"Yes?"

"Will you be my girlfriend?"

My heart soars.

"Yes."

"We're still really different people."

"I know."

"I believe in God and you don't."

"I know."

"I'm pro-life and you're not."

"I know."

He takes a breath.

"That one's a big deal. I mean, we'll do everything we can not to get pregnant. But there's a chance it could happen."

"I know. Women are used to thinking about that possibility, on account of us having uteruses."

He smiles a little. "So what would we do if that happened?"

"I don't know."

"You don't?"

I shake my head. "I have no idea. No clue. And I don't think there's any way for us to know in advance." An echo of an old discussion comes back to me. "It's kind of a Schrödinger's Cat scenario. Right now, all the possible outcomes exist at the same time. We can't know what's in the box until we get there."

Daniel is staring at me like I've grown a second head.

"What?" I ask after a moment.

"You said Schrödinger's Cat."

I nod. "It's a quantum mechanics thing."

"I know that, Tamsin. I read science books for fun." He's still holding my hand, and now his thumb strokes the back of my wrist. "Name dropping Schrödinger's Cat is like handing me a brandy on a snowy night and saying 'Baby, it's cold outside.'"

I start to smile. "It is, huh?"

"Yeah."

I lean a little closer. "Hey, Daniel?"

"What?"

"Kiss me."

His lips touch mine like butterfly wings. But before long his hands are under my shirt and his palms are on my breasts and his tongue is doing wicked, wonderful things.

I don't know how long the kiss goes on, but it's not long enough. I feel deliciously mussed afterward, and as we sit there with our arms around each other, I realize I'm smiling like a fool.

A fool in love.

"Hey, Daniel?"

"Yeah?"

"Can I tell you something sweet?"

"Yeah."

"You make me want to believe in God."

His arm tightens around my shoulders.

"Hey, Tamsin?"

"Yes?"

"I don't want to change you. On the other hand—"

"Yes?"

"I could spend my life arguing with you and die a happy man."

The melting feeling behind my breastbone is back.

"Deal."

* * *

Daniel and I aren't like Rikki and Sam. You meet the two of them and think, man, these two people belong together.

It's the same with Will and Claire. Everyone had them tagged as a couple before they finally figured things out.

Daniel and I don't fit like that. We're not a perfect match.

People said that about my grandparents. My grandfather passed away ten years ago, but my grandmother still talks about how they met and what their married life was like. He was this super-smart, hyper-intellectual English professor, and she was a seamstress who didn't even finish high school. No one thought they should get married, but they did—and they had forty happy years together.

What I said to Daniel is true. There's no way to predict the future. But as I'm sitting here with my head on his shoulder, a picture comes into my mind.

It's me, talking to my grandchildren.

They told us it would never last, I say. *And yet here we are, celebrating our fiftieth wedding anniversary.*

And this moment, I'll tell them, *is when our happily-ever-after began.*

ACKNOWLEDGEMENTS

Thanks as always to Mikel Strom and Tara Gorvine for their help, encouragement, and endless patience, and to my mother for her general awesomeness. Thanks to Sarah Hansen (Okay Creations) for her gorgeous cover. And finally, an epic thank-you to my readers, who are the reason I write.

ABOUT THE AUTHOR

Abigail Strom started writing stories at the age of seven and has never been able to stop. On her way to becoming a full-time writer, she earned a BA in English from Cornell University as well as an MFA in dance from the University of Hawaii, and held a wide variety of jobs from dance teacher and choreographer to human resource manager. Now she works in her pajamas and lives in New England with her family, who are incredibly supportive of the hours she spends hunched over her computer.

For more information, visit her at abigailstrom.com.

www.ingramcontent.com/pod-product-compliance
Lightning Source LLC
LaVergne TN
LVHW091029080826
845145LV00002B/421

* 9 7 8 1 9 4 3 2 9 6 0 6 4 *